Carrots and Miggle

Carrots and Miggle

by ARDATH MAYHAR

ATHENEUM   1986   NEW YORK

Library of Congress Cataloging-in-Publication Data

Mayhar, Ardath.
Carrots and Miggle.

SUMMARY: When Carrot's distant relative Emiglia moves
from a scholarly English home to the Ramsden ranch
in Texas, everyone has to make adjustments.
[1. Ranch life—Fiction.   2. Texas—Fiction]
I.Title.
PZ7.M468Car 1986   [Fic]   85-20024
ISBN 0-689-31184-2

*To all my fellow freaks
who are still hacking their way
through the jungle of normality.*

Contents

Carrots
and
Miggle

1
Weeds and Worms and All That Good Stuff

THERE WAS A BOBBLE IN THE WATER, AND THE BIT of stick that was serving as a float dipped sharply at one end. Carrots thrust her stub of a pencil and her grubby notebook into her denim pocket and took the cane pole in both hands. There was a perch down there, sure as shooting.

After several delicate flirtations with the sodden earthworm threaded onto the hook, the fish must have decided that this was too good a meal to share with the smaller ones of its kind that were beginning to make dashes at the treat. The stick slid under smoothly, and Carrots, with the ease of a born fisherman, pulled up and back on the pole. With a wet *shplop!* the sunperch came free of the water and swung in the sunlight, its red-gold stomach shining.

"Six!" exclaimed Carrots, satisfaction in her gruff voice. "Just about enough for a mess for Aunt Ella."

Roger's tail thumped once in agreement as she dropped the fish into the bent bucket at her side and threaded another protesting worm onto the hook. Then his ears came up, and he looked across the cattle pond. "*Rrrrooof!*" he said, with some emphasis.

Carrots followed the direction of his glance. "Uh-oh!"

Laying aside her pole, she reached backward to catch the .22 rifle leaning against the willow behind her. She jacked a cartridge into the chamber and went onto one knee among the goatweeds.

A rippling wedge of water was following the black head of a moccasin as it swam diagonally across the small pond toward the spot where the cows came down to drink twice a day. More than once a cow had been badly bitten, and that didn't do a dairy cow any good at all.

Spat! There was a boiling disturbance where the wedge-shaped head had been. Coils rose and sank, rose again, then sank to rise no more.

Carrots jacked the spent shell from the rifle and

leaned it back against the tree. Reaching out a square and grimy paw, she ruffled Roger's ears.

"Good dog! Only snake dog in captivity!"

The German shepherd grinned, his tongue lolling from the corner of his mouth, saliva dripping onto her sleeve. Neither of them minded in the least.

She squinted at the sun, now just visible above the forest beyond the water. Already its edge was below the highest rank of pine needles, but Carrots felt that she had a bit of time, still. The little lake lay in a wide saucer of land, surrounded on all sides by thickets and stands of big hickories and oaks and pines. It wasn't as late as it looked. Besides, she wasn't in any hurry to get home. Not today.

It hadn't anything to do with the long hours of work yet to be done before the day was over at Bobcat Ridge Dairy Farm. Her mother had understood, which was why she had suggested this jaunt to the perch pond. Mother understood a lot; entirely too much, at times. Not that that made her change her decisions.

Carrots sighed and pulled in another perch, larger than the last. Plopping it into her bucket, she peered into the worm can. Not a wiggle of motion. She shook it hopefully, but not even a piece of worm seemed to be left.

The ghost of a cool breeze moved across the lake, pushing ripples before it. It almost seemed chilly amid the muggy heat of an East Texas summer afternoon, and Carrots shook herself and stood. She wound the line firmly about the pole, stuck the hook into the stick-bobber, and set the whole over one shoulder, along with the .22. She hooked a spare finger into the mouth of the worm can, then lifted the sloshing bucket of water and fish.

"Come on, Roger. They'll be getting ready to milk, time we get there."

He rose from amid the goatweeds, snorted heavily to get the dusty smell out of his nose, and trotted ahead of her up the cowpath that led into the woods. Carrots squinched her bare toes in the deep powder of the dusty path, feeling the warmth all through herself. There was something about the smell of a late midsummer afternoon, the white dust, the occasional drying cowpat . . . something that ached to find a way out of her.

"How in heck can you make poetry out of worms and weeds and cowpats?" she asked aloud. It could be done. She knew that, on some deep level she hadn't any name for. It was just something she hadn't figured out how to do, yet. But she would. No question about that.

Roger knew quite well when one of her questions required an answer. This one didn't. He detoured past a rotting stump to investigate any signals that some passing fox or red wolf might have deposited there in the past couple of hours.

Carrots trudged on, deep in thought. Ahead a crow signaled her coming to anything in the woods that cared to know. For once she didn't notice and caw in return. This was one day she hated to see end. Tomorrow . . . tomorrow everything could well be changed, totally and for all time.

"It isn't that I'm selfish. I *think* it isn't that," she said to Roger, who had come up behind her.

He whuffed, feeling that this time a comment was called for.

"No, I don't mind sharing. I don't mind work . . . I like it, really. Milking, and haying, and everything. No. I just don't like changes, you know?"

"*Rowf!*"

Carrots shifted the gun and the pole on her shoulder, easing a sore spot where they'd been resting. "But maybe I'm just borrowing trouble. Maybe nothing will change. We'll go and wash up and get the milking things ready, and tonight will come and go, and nothing will change at all. That could really happen, don't you think?"

There was no reply. Carrots hadn't expected one. Even Roger knew that things were in the process of becoming strange and uncomfortable. She felt it in her bones.

2

Everything Looks Worse After Dark

BY THE TIME THE FISH HAD BEEN CLEANED AND delivered to Aunt Ella in the small house out on the road, the afternoon was definitely on its way out. Carrots sped through washing up and donning her milking clothes. Her brother's pickup was already sitting in front of the dairy barn, and she could see her mother trudging down the path toward the calf pen with a bucket of feed pellets.

The familiar routine of scouring and disinfecting the milker and the strainers took her mind off coming problems better than anything else could have. Carrots had been doing these chores since her tenth birthday, and the routine settled down like a comforting arm about her shoulders. By now she was one of the best dairymen in the county. That wasn't her own assessment. It had been said to her mother by none other than the state inspector of dairies.

"I have forty-year-old dairymen who don't do as good a job of sanitation and have higher bacteria counts than your twelve-year-old does. You and Glen may do the heavy part of the work, but when the chips are down, it's the one who does the cleaning and sterilizing who makes the difference."

Carrots had glowed quietly ever since. Dad's death had left such a huge gap in their lives and the work of the farm that every one of them had felt compelled to pitch in and do more than they had ever been able to before. But until Glen and his wife had moved into the house they'd built on the north hundred acres, it had been very hard. Mama worked to her limits, but she and Carrots together weighed less than two hundred pounds. Handling bags of feed and bales of hay, stretching fence-wire and doctoring thousand-pound animals was a lot harder job for them than it had been for Dad. If Glen hadn't decided to go back into dairying, to operate the family farm with them, they might have—Carrots gulped at the thought as her hands set a strainer in its rack and inserted the filter—might have had to sell out.

Of course, there was Cherry. She did what she could, feeding calves and bringing feed to the troughs and watching the milkers, but even if you're almost six, there just isn't much that isn't a lot too big for you to handle. She was going to be some kind of farmer, one day, but for now she just hadn't the size.

A long wail from the back gate told her that Glen was ready for the cows. She grabbed the old-fashioned double-unit milker and trundled it into the back of the barn, setting it between two stanchions and attaching its tubing to the vacuum outlet. It would be nice, someday, if they could get one of those automated set-ups. The kind that took the milk straight from the cow into a tank-type cooler. Maybe one day, if Glen did well and his wife didn't lose her job and Mama agreed. . . .

Her brother's dark-red head peered around the double doors in the back of the barn. "Feed ready?" he asked.

"Bring 'em in!" shouted Cherry from the feed room.

Half-Pint and Maggie marched sedately into the barn and turned into their accustomed places. Every pair was milked together in the same order in the same spot, morning and night. Like circus ponies, they knew the routine and seemed to enjoy it. As they chomped into the feed, Carrots attached the milkers to their freshly-washed udders. The milker began its iambic throbbing.

Ka-*cha!* Ka-*cha!* Ka-*cha!*

Carrots found a sonnet forming in her head, but she shooed it away and watched the level of feed in the troughs, the rise of milk in the container, and the approach of the next pair of animals, who knew their turn was coming up. Mama came in through the feed room window and checked the ration in the next double stanchion.

"Just right," she called back to Cherry, who was coming through the door with her fat hands burdened with two more buckets. She dumped them into another set of troughs.

Now the routine was settling in. Every member of the family moved in a prescribed pattern of motions, doing his or her own task with ease and smoothness. Sometimes Carrots thought the best time of the day was the evening milking. Not morning; she hated getting up early and always had and always would, she felt certain. But in the evening it was lovely, if it wasn't raining, or the cows weren't upset by the wolf pack that ranged across the abandoned farm to the east, or the lights didn't go out because of a rainstorm.

She felt the tension going out of her. Everything would be all right. Surely it would! Maybe there would be a call when they got up to the house, and nothing would change, after all.

It was after eight when she finished cleaning the equipment and washing the floors. Glen had already gone home to Cissie and his little Chuck. Mama had gone down to turn the calves out into the pasture for the night. Cherry had tagged after her, for she was a bit afraid of the gathering dark. Carrots liked finishing up, turning out the light, and moving up the track toward the house.

Everything was invisible in the dark. Only the sky, showing its first stars, was full of splendor. She walked absentmindedly, letting her feet find their own way. Her eyes were on the sky, as they usually were when it wasn't raining or the moon wasn't too bright.

"I walk up a road of stars . . ." she murmured, feeling as if the bright path of the Milky Way lay below her feet instead of infinitely above her head. Her foot hit a rut and she stumbled, fell from her starry road into the mundane trail, and found the back gate at hand.

This was the time she had dreaded. "Some time around eight-thirty," Grandaunt Lizzie had said. "I'll call you to let you know if this is necessary. By then all the facts will be in hand, and the child will have been consulted."

Ugh! Carrots felt something warm and bitter rise in her throat. She didn't want anyone else to come and disrupt the regular rhythm of her days. Mama might have the care of her, washing and cooking and such, but it was Carrots who would have the newcomer tagging around after her.

She leaned her forehead against the porch post, feeling the warm, blistered paint scratch against her skin. "What kind of person gets named Emiglia?" she asked Roger, who was dozing on the mat. "What kind of person has a name that ends in *wiescz?*" She shuddered. She'd given up on trying to figure out that name the first time she'd seen it written. Mama, recalling from her childhood the language of her grandparents, had sailed through the many-syllabled thing with ease. Carrots never expected to be able to.

Roger thumped his tail against the screen door, begging to go in with her. She grunted at him, and he settled back onto the mat as she stepped up into the back bedroom. In the dark she pulled off her smelly milking clothes and hung them to air before being washed. Still without turning on a light, she went into the bath and washed thoroughly. Her light summer caftan went over her head, and then she ran her fingers through her short, springy hair.

Only then did she turn on a light to inspect herself. Mama insisted on her being tidy for supper. As she looked into the fogged mirror, the telephone rang.

She scuffed her feet into sandals and hurried through the hallway into the kitchen. Her mother stood by the telephone. One hand was stirring something on the stove; the other held the instrument to her ear. Her eyes looked faraway and very sad.

"Yes, I understand. Tell Emiglia that I feel for her. . . . I hope the service was of some comfort to her. I wish that I could have come when Camilla died, but I'm sure you understand our circumstances. Yes. Yes. Indeed, we're looking forward to having her come to stay with us."

Her eyes met Carrots's, and her look challenged her daughter to say truthfully that she wasn't ready to welcome someone who had lost both her parents in so short a time. Carrots felt tears behind her eyelids.

What if she had lost Dad, and then Mama, too?

A dreadful thought. As if the world ended without warning. But still. . . .

She took plates from the cupboard, silverware from the drawer, set the table for three. Soon it would be four!

When Mama hung up the phone, she took the pot of dumplings and set it onto the counter. As they served themselves, her expression was odd. Sad, of course, but excited, too.

"Well, girls," she said, dipping in with the big ladle, "it looks as if you're going to have a new sister."

Cherry, too young to realize what that might mean, jumped up and down with excitement. Carrots looked above her bobbing head toward Mama. Mama's eyes had that look. That shape-up-or-else look.

Carrots managed a feeble grin. "Whoopee!" she croaked.

3

And Even Worse
in the Rain

THE CLOCK WENT OFF WITH ITS USUAL MIND-JARRING jangle. Carrots turned over and reached blindly for the button to silence it. Beside her, Cherry stirred and grumbled sleepily, then burrowed her head into the pillow and zonked out again.

In the dark (her brother insisted that Carrots must be part owl because she liked to get about without turning lights on), she felt sleepily for her slippers. By the time she was standing, she was awake enough to realize that it was raining. Pouring, to be exact.

Drat!

Naturally, she didn't say it aloud, for Mama disapproved of such expressions, and she was moving about in the bathroom just next door. But this was too much. First the bad news. Now this. A drippy cow was no fun at all to wash and milk, and it was entirely too hot to wear a slicker.

A dash into the bathroom, dragging on fresh coveralls, a quick cup of hot tea, and Carrots found herself following Mama's squishy steps toward the dairy barn. Wind was gusting from the northwest, which gave some promise that this rain would pass over in a bit. That was something—but not much.

It was a messy milking. Warm trickles of drip from the cows' backs fell into Carrots's fiery curls, making them hang limply about her face. Great care had to be taken to wash not only the cows' udders but their entire middles, which only added to the time she must spend beneath the big bellies, sponge in hand. By the time the morning milking was over, she felt grungy and out of sorts with the world.

The rain settled into a light drizzle by breakfast time, and Carrots felt her spirits begin to rise, rather against her will. It would stop in a while, and the sun would blaze forth and make the whole world steam, she knew.

The phone rang.

Mama turned from this call with her figuring-

out-the-schedule look on her face. "That was Aunt
Lizzie. Emiglia will be on the four o'clock plane—
they were able to make connections in Dallas with
the local airline, so we won't have to make that long
drive. Just over to Larkin. That's a relief! But it will
put me late for milking. Can you manage, Sweet
Stuff?"

Carrots wanted to say, "Anything at all to keep
from having to smile and look as if I'm glad to see
a cousin I never heard of three weeks ago!" But she
didn't. She poured milk over her cereal and stirred it
carefully.

"Sure. No problem. Cherry can tend to the little
calves—it's not nearly so much trouble in the evening
when the big ones aren't with them. Tell . . . tell
Emiglia I'm sorry about her mom." That choked her
a bit, but it got out.

Mama smiled. "I think I'll go early and get
groceries and gas up the car. That'll save a trip later
in the week. We can finish getting the extra room
ready this morning, and then after I'm gone you and
Cherry can pick the late tomatoes and check for peas
on the vines. I noticed yesterday that the new crop
of blackeyes is coming on, blooming like mad. We'll
get the rest of the freezer full, at this rate."

Carrots took a bite of cereal. It had been too

much to hope for that today would include another trip to the perch pond. But maybe, if things went smoothly, she could ease off into the woods for a half hour before milking. Somehow the woods made her feel better, no matter what. Would they do the same with a stranger dogging her footsteps? The thought came suddenly, and it left her feeling dreary.

It was a busy day. When Mama had something to do, she went at it hammer and tongs. Anyone helping her had to move speedily or get stepped on, too. The extra room looked, for a time, as if a tornado were sweeping through it, removing curtains, flopping mattress and pillows, whisking on sheets, polishing up the good old furniture until it gleamed.

"Faster than a speeding bullet . . ." muttered Carrots, as she glanced over their handiwork. The room looked as if Emiglia had been expected for weeks instead of hours.

Cherry bustled past, squeezing her sister against the doorframe. In her arms was a giant panda, almost as large as she. It had been a gift from her godmother, but the child had hesitated to share her affection with it and chance hurting her old Teddy's feelings. She never played with it.

She thumped it onto the bed, against the ruffled

pillows. "Maybe Pud will make her feel better. He's good to cuddle, but don't tell Teddy that!"

Carrots grinned. Maybe Cherry had the right idea. They couldn't do anything about the situation. Why not enjoy it? Probably Emiglia was just as upset and unhappy at the way things were going as anyone else could be. Still. . . .

"Lunch!" Mama said, herding her daughters from the room and closing the door against dust. "By the time we're done, it'll be time for me to scoot. Good thing this happened this week. Next week the big hayfield will be ready to cut. That might have made problems."

Before Carrots was ready, she was watching the tail of dust follow Mama's Chevy down the half mile of bumpy driveway toward the road. It was actually about to happen!

She looked down at Cherry. The big brown eyes were droopy. She had better take a nap before they tackled the garden.

She looked down the drive again. You'd think, with all that rain, it wouldn't be dusty so quickly. But the big milk truck and the sun, between them, had dried things out fast. That was the way—nothing seemed to go by sensible rules.

While Cherry napped, Carrots sat at the long library table that served as their eating table in the kitchen, her stub of pencil in hand, her notebook before her. She badly needed to get some things onto paper. She didn't quite know what they were, and when you wrote, you needed to know what you were doing. Just putting one word after another wasn't going to accomplish much. It had to mean something.

Today our cousin Emiglia whatever-it-is-wiescz is coming to live with us, she began. So far, so good. *It is sort of a shock to us, as we've never met her. But we're the only kin in this country who're able to take her. All the aunts and such are very old or not too well. She was born in Belgrade and lived there just a few months. Then her parents had to leave because her father wrote something the government didn't like. He took his family to London, and they've been there ever since. Cousin Andrei died a year ago. His wife, Camilla, kept on in England, but she was getting ready to come to this country when she got sick.*

Carrots read over what she'd written. That seemed over-long for a paragraph, she thought. Time to start another. One day she'd get it firmly in mind when to end one.

Great-aunt Lizzie had made all the legal arrange-

*ments for them, and she sent them money to fly to
New York three months ago. They did, and all
the imi—immi?—gration papers got fixed up before
Cousin Camilla got too sick to tend to things. Three
days ago Camilla died.*

Carrots stared down at the pencilled words. It
was so simple to write them. Easy as falling off a log.
But those few words had upset the lives of a lot of
people. Most of all, she suspected, the girl who was
in a plane zooming over the pine forests of East
Texas.

With a sigh she took up her task. *Mama has gone
to meet the plane. Great-aunt Lizzie seemed really
upset at having to ask us to take Emiglia. I think she
wanted to keep her herself, but when you're eighty-
two that's not too practical. She knows it's been hard
for us since Dad died. There's a lot of work and not
much money. But she's going to send a bit, when she
can, to help out with expenses. And Mama . . . well,
Mama never turned down anybody in her life. Not
if they really needed her.*

*I wonder if I'll ever be as good a person as Mama?
She never seems to mind when people take up her
time and her energy, no matter how busy she is on
the farm. I resent it!* She looked at the line and under-
lined the word resent. *I want to do my work, go to*

*school in winter. Wander around in the woods or
fish in the pond or sit in the brush and write poetry.
I don't want to be* BOTHERED *with some stranger who
is all upset from losing her entire family and will need
a lot of sympathy and coddling. Besides, she's from
the city. That's going to be a problem, I just know it!*

*I just don't know. I'll do my best. But I just do
not know.*

Cherry pattered into the kitchen, her eyes puffy
with sleep. "We better go." She yawned. "Want to
be finished when Mama and Miggle get here."

Carrots laughed. "It's Ay-meeg-lee-ah," she said,
giving it Mama's pronunciation.

"Too much trouble. Miggle's easier," said
Cherry.

From long experience with the hardness of her
sister's head, Carrots had the uneasy suspicion that her
new cousin would very likely find herself to be Miggle forever. Not too bad, actually. Not nearly as bad
as Emiglia.

"Well, Miggle or not, we'd better pop our coat-
tails to the garden, or Mama will have something to
say when she gets back," Carrots observed, putting
her straw hat onto her blazing curls and cramming
Cherry's onto her black braids.

They took two big baskets into their calloused

hands, picked up their snake-sticks, then set out into the hot afternoon. But Carrots wasn't thinking about the task. Her mind was on a plane, drawing nearer and nearer to Larkin.

"I don't care. I HATE it!" something inside her was insisting.

4
Miggle

IT WAS HOT IN THE GARDEN, SET IN A CLEARED BRIAR patch in the middle of a pine thicket. Though the breeze sounded deliciously cool as it whooshed through the pine-tops, the thick stand of trees kept any of it from reaching those who worked among the tomato plants. Besides, the rain of the morning had only made the steamy heat worse after the sun came out.

Cherry stood and wiped her sweaty forehead on her shirt-tail. "I'm just about burned *up!*" she panted. "We about have all the ripe ones, Carrots?"

Carrots straightened her own kinked back. "Two more plants to go on this row. Then I'll help you with the rest of yours. Hold on another ten minutes, and I think we'll be done with it. For today. It's all got to be done again tomorrow."

Cherry groaned dramatically and dived into a tangle of vines. The late tomatoes had done better than well, and both girls were burdened with heavy basket loads when they headed for home.

The house was cool, for they had left the ceiling fans on to stir the air. The bare pine floors were cool to their feet, once they took off the boots they wore in the overgrown garden. Not only copperheads lurked there; sometimes stumptail moccasins found their way into the cool vines from the stream that meandered at the bottom of the slope behind the pines.

Carrots looked at the clock. "Almost four," she said. The plane would soon be arriving.

Cherry emerged from the bathroom, dripping water from face and arms. "I'm starving to death!" she announced.

Her sister groaned. "When did I ever see you when you weren't?" But she rummaged in the refrigerator and got the funny old-fashioned pot with a lid that held Mama's own special homemade mayonnaise. She washed a couple of sun-warmed tomatoes under the faucet, rinsing away the dust. Then she sliced thick rounds onto some spread bread. The two sat to bite into tomato sandwiches.

Cherry sighed. "There's nothing in the world better!" she said. "Not chicken and dressing at Christmas. Not Mama's fudge cake. Nothing."

Carrots, tasting the rich, fruity juice as it oozed through the bread and mayo, could only agree. "I'll bet Miggle—Emiglia, I mean—never tasted anything that good in London," she said.

The sound of Glen's arrival on the tractor hurried them into tidying the table and making for their coveralls. When Glen returned from his work in the fields and on the fencelines, it was a sure sign that milking time was at hand. With Mama gone, it meant that the girls must attend to all the preliminaries, so they hastened to the barn and the feed room. But Carrots found her ear tuned to the scanty traffic on the road some half mile from the house. Mama would be here before too long. With Miggle.

She found her stomach performing uncomfortable acrobatics as she measured the disinfectant into the cleaning water, checked the rubber parts of the milkers, and leaned halfway into the five-gallon milk container looking for traces of milkstone. As she surfaced, she heard the unmistakable sound of the

Chevy coming up the winding hill out of their front woods.

Something fiercely proud and stiff inside her kept her from running to the door to look out. "I'm doing my work!" she muttered to herself. "It helps support the whole family. That comes first!" But something else she couldn't quite define also held her to her task.

She could hear Cherry giving little hoots of excitement as she pelted toward the house. That was fine; Cherry was only five, after all.

Glen's rubber boots squeaked on the wet cement floor as he came to the door of the milk room and peeped into the white-painted chamber where the milk was strained and cooled. "Not going up to see our new kin?" he asked. "I thought you'd be racing Cherry."

She looked into the brown eyes that were almost identical to her own. And to Dad's . . . but she pushed that thought aside.

"I don't mean to be ugly, Bruh," she said, scrubbing blindly at a strainer. "But I . . . I just don't like this. Something bothers me a lot. So I can wait until after milking to see what's-'er-name. And then some."

He opened the screen door and came to stand beside her, looking down from his six-foot height with concern. "Listen, Babe, this isn't going to be dead easy for any of us. You know as well as I do that money's tight right now. Even with some help from Aunt Lizzie, it's going to put a strain on us to have somebody else to feed and clothe and keep well and in school. Mama's going to get the worst of it, 'cause she's the one Emiglia is going to expect to straighten things out for her. And think about Emiglia—she's not a happy girl right now, you can bet your boots on that."

Carrots shook her head fiercely to get rid of the tears that had come to her eyes. "I know. I've said it all to myself, a lot of times. I'll be okay. Don't worry. I'll figure it out someway."

He patted her on the shoulder, very gently. It was so like the way Dad used to do that another tear came sliding down her nose. But he said nothing else and went to call the first cows, who were lowing to him just over the hill.

Milking went entirely too quickly. Long before she was ready to face the new situation, Carrots found herself walking toward the house. Not watching stars; not tonight! Not thinking of lines of poetry. Dreading.

As she reached the back gate, Mama snapped on the porch light and stepped onto the back porch. "There you are! It's been a long day, hasn't it? And I want you to meet Emiglia."

As she moved into the fan of light, Carrots saw her cousin for the first time. Emiglia was small-boned but rather tall for eleven. Her hair had that same raven-wing gloss that Mama's and Cherry's did, but her face was thin and colorless. To avoid looking into her eyes, Carrots studied her clothing.

Ugh!

She wore a dark blue blazer over a white shirt. A blue-gray plaid skirt came to her knees, and below that, heat or not, she wore black stockings and strapped shoes. She didn't look American, not at all. And there was something about the way she stood that said, "This is the only proper way to dress!"

Carrots felt her lip curl. She'd like to see Miggle try dressing like that in the hayfield. Or milking old Clara, who kicked you whenever she felt like it. The notion made her grin, in spite of herself, and she looked up to meet the stranger's gaze.

Two black eyes were staring into hers, and they were filled with complete hostility.

For a moment that felt terribly long, Carrots stood quite still, stunned by the dislike and disapproval she read in the face of the newcomer. Then Emiglia turned to Mama.

"You allow your daughter to go about like *that?* As if she were some . . . some *laborer?*"

Carrots felt her face growing warm with anger. She held onto her temper as well as she could, but she wasn't about to take that from anybody.

"I am a laborer," she said quietly. "We all labor here. That's the way we make our living. We're farmers, just like our dad and his dad before him. It's not like Europe here—you're not stuck with other people's labels if you don't want to be. If you respect yourself, others will respect you."

Mama's quick smile flashed across the space between them. Carrots knew she hadn't overreacted.

She watched wonderingly as Miggle curled her lip. A sudden cruel light shone in her eyes as she said, "My father would call you a *peasant!*"

Carrots glanced at Mama. Mama was frowning, a tiny twitch of wrinkle between her brows. She nodded slightly.

"My father would call you ill-bred," Carrots said, turning to the bathroom. But once in the tub of warm water she wondered. Miggle had been reared by strict rules of conduct. How had she forgotten herself so far as to say what she had said? Could it be that she was dreading Carrots as much as Carrots had dreaded her? Or was she merely in shock, after the loss of her last close relative?

As she scrubbed and rinsed, Carrots puzzled over it. But she had seen that wild spark in her cousin's eye. It might well be pure grief, a lashing out at the world in anger at her loss.

She devoutly hoped so, for all their sakes.

5

More Miggle

CARROTS STAYED IN THE BATH UNTIL HER SKIN BEGAN shriveling from the water. Then, very reluctantly, she dressed in her caftan and sandals and went into the kitchen to supper. Not that she was hungry. She felt as if a bite of anything at all would make her terribly sick. But it was the thing she had to do. It wouldn't be fair to Mama and Cherry if she didn't. She had seen the way Miggle looked at them, too. It hadn't been admiration she had seen in those black eyes.

The table was set. A roasted chicken was steaming in its middle, surrounded by boiled corn and fresh green beans and sliced tomatoes. The smell made Carrots want to upchuck, but she held on to herself and went to her place.

Emiglia was sitting on the side of the long table that was up against the row of windows. Dad had made a bench exactly the right length for that side, and everyone always wanted to sit there. As Carrots slipped into her chair at the end of the table, Emiglia's dark head came up.

"I must . . . apologize to you for my words. I am over-tired and upset. This is a new country to me, and your ways are totally different from any I have ever known. I hope that you will forgive me." There was nothing wrong with the words, except for the fact that they sounded as if the speaker should be a forty-year-old schoolteacher. The tone, however, left Carrots puzzled. It hadn't matched the words.

But Mama was smiling with relief as she poured tall glasses of cold milk and set the homemade bread out. "There. That's better. We've got to pull together here and get along. It isn't easy for strangers to have to live together. . . ." She passed slices of bread about. "And work together."

Carrots noted that Miggle gave a small jerk when Mama mentioned work.

"Now you're here, Emiglia, and we're glad to have you." Mama took up her fork.

"Cousin Ginevra," said Miggle, pushing a bit of chicken about on her plate, her fork in her left hand, "I do appreciate your taking me in. Never did I expect to be one of those unfortunates in the books, orphaned and without any recourse. My cousin Lizaveta in New York was more than kind, but I am sure that you know her condition. When she told me that I might come here to Texas and be with your family, I cried with thankfulness."

Mama beamed. "Do call me Ginny, dear. Everyone does, unless they call me Mama. And that's enough of doleful talk for tonight. We're all too tired to cope with serious things. Let's finish our supper and read a bit before bedtime. Have a nice quiet evening. Tomorrow we can begin getting you settled in."

Supper did end quietly, much to Carrots's relief. She found, when she applied herself, that the lump in her throat had disappeared, and the chicken and vegetables went down smoothly. When Mama brought out an ice-cream-strawberry pie she had bought in Larkin, there was no question of its eager reception.

Afterward, Cherry turned on the TV and found a good old movie. She and Miggle sat on the long sofa, but Carrots didn't think Miggle paid too much attention to the program. Not that she, Carrots,

glanced up from her book all that often. Mama had
brought her the copy of *Modern American Poets* that
she had saved her money for for so long. She was
alternately savoring well-turned lines and frowning
at what she considered to be deliberate obscurity most
of the evening.

"Charlotte!"

Emiglia's voice had to repeat the name before
Carrots remembered it was the one Mama and Dad
had given her.

"Sorry!" She looked up to find Emiglia watching her closely. "I've been called Carrots for so long
that when anyone says, 'This is Charlotte Ramsden,'
I hardly know they mean me. Though it will be a
good name for a poet, if and when I succeed in becoming one."

Miggle wasn't paying much attention to her
words. "Ginny said that you would show me to my
room and help me to get settled. Would you mind?
I am terribly tired."

"Sure! Come on. G'night, Mama. Cherry, you
coming? We might as well all go together. I'm about
ready, anyway."

The three girls went up the narrow stair to the
bedrooms in single file, Carrots leading the way.
Miggle had been given the east bedroom, across the

hall from the one shared by Carrots and Cherry. Its
door was open. A cool breeze swept across the hall,
carrying with it the fresh scent of the hayfield that
Glen had mowed that morning, together with the
voices of a million and one crickets and frogs and that
of a whippoorwill mourning in the woods.

"That sound . . . what is it?" asked Emiglia,
her eyes wide in her pale face. "Some beast of the
forest?"

Carrots felt a rush of empathy. For an instant she
felt as Miggle must feel, and all the familiar sounds
and scents were suddenly alien to her, strange and
threatening. Far off, probably at the perch pond
where she had fished, the shrill cries of the wolf pack
pricked the night with sharp sounds. She looked
quickly at Miggle, but she was evidently unable to
distinguish that sound from the harmless ones of the
peepers and grasshoppers.

"Just a whippoorwill, a kind of night bird.
You'll hear them often around here. They love the
woods. All those other sounds are just little creatures
in the grass and shrubbery and the swampy spot in
the front woods. Not one thing to be uneasy about.
You're safer right here than almost anyplace—particularly someplace full of people, like New York or
London."

The girl before her relaxed. Carrots could see the tense shoulders soften, the forehead lose its line of worry.

"You remember where the bathroom is? The big one downstairs has a tub. Our little one up here just has a shower. You've got everything you need? Good. Mama sleeps in the downstairs back bedroom, just in case you want her for anything."

With a smile, Carrots left her cousin to her own devices and followed Cherry into their room. She had a suspicion that Miggle wasn't nearly as composed as she seemed. If, in the middle of the night, she came unglued, Carrots felt sure she'd want Mama, not a strange cousin a year older than herself.

For once the night was cool. Dad had thought long and hard about air-conditioning, before he died, but there hadn't been enough money. And then there was the terrible shock to your system when you came from hundred-degree-plus heat into such unnatural coolness. So the house was filled with natural air and the noises of the night. Nice, for Miggle's first night here. The next real swelterer they had, she'd have a hard time of it. Along with the rest of the family.

She'd thought she wouldn't sleep too much, but Carrots went off as quickly as Cherry. Her dreams were full of uneasy things she couldn't quite grasp

before they were gone, however, and she woke to
pitch blackness, her bones feeling uneasy.

Maybe a glass of water would help. She got up
and padded down the hall to the half-bath. Miggle
had left her door open a crack to let the breeze
through. And from it came the unmistakable sound
of a muffled sob behind the door.

Carrots paused in the hall. For the first time in
her life, she found herself feeling what another person must be undergoing. What if she had lost Mama?
A terrible sick pain filled her, along with a feeling of
emptiness. What a lonely world it must seem for
Emiglia, right now. Surrounded by strangers whose
ways were totally alien to her. No wonder she had
lashed out at them.

Carrots wondered if she should go in and try to
comfort the girl, but she remembered something she'd
read in one of Mama's magazines. People needed to
grieve, to cry, to get it out of their systems. It was
probably best for Miggle to cry it all out, now. She
had been hiding all that pain entirely too well. Anger,
she knew, burned you up from the inside. Maybe the
tears would wash out much of that.

She stood there for a moment. Then she yawned.
Probably it was best to let it be. She crept to the bathroom, then back to bed.

Lying there waiting for sleep, she thought deeply. Life with Miggle wasn't going to be easy. Even this soon she found herself both liking and disliking the girl. Liking her for her stiff upper lip, but disliking her for her instant contempt for a way of life she didn't even know.

She almost dozed off. Then her eyes opened wide. Miggle was going to have to do some fast growing-up to make it here. But it had just occurred to Carrots that she was going to have to do the same. She was going to have to think of end results, not her own feelings. Dad had told her that many times, but only now did she understand what it was that he'd meant.

So. She sighed, turned on her side, and drifted off to sleep.

6
The Doomfuls

THOUGH CARROTS HAD GONE TO SLEEP WITH THE BEST of resolutions for the next day, she woke to a feeling of heaviness and gloom. She trudged through the early morning dimness toward the dairy barn, her mood getting worse with every step; and though she understood what was happening, she seemed powerless to stop it.

Dad had called it "the doomfuls." He, too, had been subject to fits of depression, and at those times his temper, which matched his red hair, had been set at hair-trigger pressure.

"Fight it," he'd told her frequently. "I've been wrestling that Irish temper of mine for as long as I can remember, and I still have a long way to go. You can start now, young and fresh, and maybe get it under control by the time you're my age."

Carrots had taken his words to heart, for the blind black rage that would sometimes descend on her always left her shaken and sick to her stomach, maybe for days. This morning she felt as if she were a gun, aimed and loaded, just ready for an excuse to go off.

Ahead of her Mama turned off to the right, heading for the big hay barn where the calf feed was kept. She really should talk to Mama about the way she felt, but Mama was calm and unruffled all the time. Carrots suspected that her mother did, indeed, suffer from sadness and anger, but if so she locked it inside.

Only Dad had truly understood what it was to be carried entirely away by anger.

Carrots gritted her teeth, flicked on the light, bringing the dead-white interior of the milk room to brilliance. Disinfect, scour, heat water, set strainers on milk cans. Always the same routine. Sometimes she couldn't remember whether this particular memory was from today or yesterday or two weeks ago. In the grip of the doomfuls she hated her work as much as she loved it the rest of the time.

As if sensing her mood, the cows were languid and uncooperative. Glen, who had his own knowledge of the doomfuls, noted the lack of banter immediately. "Not again!" his expression said as plainly as words.

That made Carrots even angrier. She hadn't done anything . . . not one thing! And here they were shrugging and twitching their eyebrows at each other, Glen and Mama. Still, milking went along smoothly, until they were almost through.

Then Clara, the big pale Jersey, rolled one white-rimmed eye back toward the point along her side where Carrots was putting the milker on her. With a motion you'd think too swift for such a big creature, she lashed out with her sharp-tipped hoof and knocked Carrots in one direction and the milker cups in the other.

Rage burst into full bloom as Carrots picked herself up from under Rosa's belly and retrieved the milker cups. Even as she took them into her hand, she felt the dark tide closing over her.

Glen's strong hands caught her by the shoulders and shook her, hard. "Carrots! Charlotte Ramsden, you come out of that!" His voice was very like Dad's when he was upset. Carrots pushed at the black mist, struggled to bring herself back down from the height to which her anger had carried her. She felt sick to her stomach, drained of strength, and sticky with sweat, all at once.

Her face was hot as she found herself once more, milker in hand, standing between Clara and Rosa, with Glen looming over her.

"You all right now?" he asked, his voice gruff.

She swallowed the taste of bile. "I . . . guess so. I wish Dad . . ."

"So do we all, believe me. Sometimes we need him badly . . . well, you just don't know. Or maybe you know better than any of us. But now we'd better get along. Clara's almost out of feed."

Any break in the rhythm and timing of the milking process always made problems. Carrots bent and washed the milker in the bucket of disinfectant that stood between each pair of stanchions. As she put the milker onto the now quiet cow, a pain shot through her forehead. It was familiar. She knew she'd have that until she settled down from her upset.

By the time the morning milking and cleaning were done, she felt a bit better. Lugging a jar of cold milk that they'd set into the cooler overnight, she went up the track toward the house. In the pits as she had been, she had almost forgotten Miggle. Her stomach gave a lurch. Just what she needed!

But things seemed quiet as she went in to breakfast. Mama, who always left the barn in time to have the meal ready for Carrots when she finished cleaning up, was dishing up a plate of scrambled eggs. Crisp bacon was laid in a pattern on the bacon plate, which had been Dad's grandmother's. On the table sat the pancake tray, its transparent cover misted with steam from the hotcakes inside. Miggle and Cherry sat on the bench, waiting with hungry expressions on their faces.

Carrots forced herself to smile. She knew that even now her cousin was assessing her clean work clothes and deciding that they, too, were those of a peasant. Not that it mattered. At the moment the main thing was to keep her stomach on an even keel. And, of course, her temper well in hand. She still felt sore and strained, and she knew that any snide remarks from Emiglia might well set her off again.

She took her place and reached out to turn the teapot spout so that it didn't point toward her. She'd always had a thing about being stared at by teapot spouts, lengths of pipe, and such. The action seemed to reassure her mother, who looked at her sharply as she set the eggs on the table and slid into her own chair.

"Have at it, chums. Today we rake the east field
and begin baling. It's a fair day, but scattered showers
are predicted for tomorrow, so we'd better make hay
while the sun shines, in the most literal sense possible." Mama smiled up the table toward Carrots.

Though her tummy threatened rebellion a couple of times, Carrots did eat. Cherry, however, noticed the odd way Miggle handled her silverware.

"You keep your fork in your left hand," she
noted. "Why? We use our right hands. See?"

Mama interrupted with, "That's the proper way
in Europe. This is the proper way here. I think the
entire idea must have been to keep people from el-
bowing each other when they sat together at a long
table. Here there's plenty of room, so there's no problem. Eat, my child. You've got to pick the peas this
morning, while we work in the hay. Emiglia can help
you. It's too soon to get her out into the heat; she's
not acclimated yet. When she gets too hot, you let
her go sit in the shade while you finish. And take
water with you—the small jug is under the sink.
Okay?"

Cherry mopped up the last of her syrup with
the final bit of pancake. "Okay. Miggle, you'll need
a big wide hat. You got one?"

Emiglia looked at her small cousin with astonishment on her face. "What is a *Miggle?*" she asked with disdain.

Mama looked at Cherry, who swallowed her last bits too fast and had to cough. Then she said, "Well, Emiglia is so long and hard to say. I think Miggle is better. Nicer, too. Nicknames are friendlier, don't you think?"

Emiglia stared for a moment, then lifted her gaze to Mama. "It is a custom?" she asked, a bit skeptically.

"I'd say it's just about the most entrenched habit in this country. They nickname the president himself. One without a nickname is usually a person people dislike."

"Oh." Miggle looked thoughtful for a minute. Then she smiled, her sallow face brightening more than Carrots had seen it do so far.

"Then I shall be Miggle. But how does one pick peas? And where?"

"Cherry will show you. She's been doing this since she was shorter than the pea vines. Listen to her—she knows where it's snaky and where the wasps nest and how to tell poison ivy from Virginia creeper. There are things that can be uncomfortable, if you don't know about them. Don't worry about wild animals. Though there are many in our woods, they won't come out to bother people, if people don't go in to bother them. See?"

Miggle nodded, but she looked almost as gloomy as Carrots felt.

"I have no hat except for the one I wear to church," she said.

Carrots shook off her lethargy. "I have two. You can have the one with the scarf that holds it on, if you want. The scarf is pink, and that doesn't do a thing for my red hair."

For the first time Miggle looked at her without active dislike in her eyes. "Thank you," she said. "And perhaps one day I, too, will go and make hay, do you think?"

That was the most encouraging thing Carrots had heard all day. "I wouldn't be surprised," she answered, sliding from her chair and helping Mama clear the table.

The dishes went into the sink to soak until there was time for washing up. Carrots found the hat, equipped Miggle with a snake stick and a basket, and waved the two pea pickers off down the shaded path.

As she turned to help Mama load the water tank onto the raking tractor that sat in the side yard, she thought of the thing she had heard the night before.

"Mama, Miggle cried in the night. Hard. I didn't

go in . . . I thought she might not want me to. I thought about calling you, but I decided not to."

Mama tucked her leather gloves into the belt of her jeans and climbed to the tractor seat. "Good thinking. Crying is a good thing, when you've been through what Emiglia has. Now open the gate. Hay waits for no man, woman, or girl."

As they chugged up the track toward the east field, Carrots clung onto the back of Mama's metal perch and flexed her knees to the bumping of the tow bar that she stood on. She was thinking hard and letting her body cope with physical things.

I'm growing up, maybe, she was thinking. *And just maybe I'll get the old temper down before too long. I wonder if it would have happened so soon if Dad*—but there she stopped. No amount of growing up and self-control would be worth the loss of her father.

7

Hay Weather
Is Hot Weather

GLEN WAS ALREADY IN THE HAYFIELD WITH THE BIG automatic baler. That was one thing Dad had scrimped for and managed to buy. Carrots could remember quite clearly going to the hayfield when she was not much bigger than Cherry and punching baling wire through the slots in the block, while Mama tied out bales and Glen and Dad forked hay into the old hay press. This was so much faster, not to mention easier, that it saved them a lot of hay every year.

Already the day was hot, though the sun was just above the treetops. Glen hooked the small tractor to the side-delivery rake—it looked like a mad spider's array of sprangly wheels—and Mama took off with

a roar, leaving a neat row of hay to follow her ma-
neuvers about the field. When she'd gone several hundred yards, Glen cranked the big tractor that pulled
the baler and lifted Carrots onto its seat. She put it
into gear and moved off, very slowly, hearing the
regular *rumble-rumble-chunk!* of the machinery as
it gobbled hay into its front and spat firm bales out
its side.

After a while, on the back leg of her journey
about the field, Carrots saw Glen picking up bales
and stacking them onto his pickup, while the neigh-
bor's son drove it along slowly beside the row of
bales. By now Mama had a regular snakes' convention
of windrow swirling in strange patterns about the
field, following the terraces and the contours of the
ground. The small tractor could take angles and steep
spots with ease, but the baler could not, being top-
heavy. So Mama made certain that the hay was rowed
in places that would pose no threat to either baler or
Carrots. More than one driver had been smashed beneath a tractor that overturned on uneven ground.

The smell of the dried hay was sweet and sneezy.
Carrots had always loved it, as well as the crackles of
grasshoppers that exploded from beneath the front
wheels as she drove along. Ahead of her a disgruntled
coachwhip slid through the grass and over the wind-

row, its black length looking exactly like the whip
it was named after. Carrots felt a quiver in her back-
bone. She did hate snakes, no matter what their habits
or usefulness.

The sun moved up the sky. The field was now
half windrow and half neat rectangles of baled hay.
Sweat poured down Carrots's back and forearms,
even puddled in her moccasins. Her face felt three
sizes too big, flushed with heat. In the sky three
cotton-ball clouds had come drifting along, and she
longed for one of them to drag its shadow across her,
just for a minute or two. It didn't.

She turned at the end of the field for the ump-
teenth time and saw Mama waiting for her in the
shade of the big cedar that formed the corner of the
field. That meant the raking was done, and Mama
would take over on the baler. Relief filled Carrots's
whole being. Another hour of moving at such a slow
rate, not even making a breeze with her passing, and
she would have been cooked to the bone.

"How goes it?" Mama asked, as the tractor
grunted to a stop beside her. "About ready for a
break? I thought you might go back to the house and
fix some lunch. It's going to be noon in less than an
hour, and we're all getting ready for a bite, I think.
You can check on Cherry and Miggle, too. I'm a little

uneasy at having to leave them alone, with Miggle so new to this country."

"Sounds good to me," Carrots replied, leaping down off the high wheel of the tractor. "I'll make about two gallons of iced tea. You want anything special, or shall I just slice the cold chicken and a lot of tomatoes and the leftover ham?"

"That'll be fine. Sandwiches are all anybody needs when it's this hot, anyway." Mama put the tractor in gear and thumped away, leaving a wake of hay bales behind her.

The walk through the woods felt cool, in contrast to the heat of the field. Carrots didn't dawdle, but she didn't miss anything, either. She saw a terrapin trundling along through the layers of dead leaves beneath the undergrowth. She noted a woodpecker nest on the underside of the huge branch some twenty feet up an oak. She jeered at the crows who heralded her coming and going. There was never enough time in the woods. Given her choice, Carrots would have built herself a nest, as the squirrels did, and lived there permanently . . . except in the winter.

Emerging from the cool greenness, she went up the winding drive toward the house, feeling again the piercing heat of the sun on her back. Yes, a couple of gallons of iced tea wouldn't be a bit too much, she was thinking, when she saw a small shape come flying from the side door and around to the front gate of the yard.

"Hurry!" shouted Cherry. "Miggle got stung!"

Oh, drat!

Carrots broke into a run, and in a moment she was standing in the kitchen doorway. Miggle sat at the table. She was sobbing, and the tears were running down a face that even she would not have recognized.

"Wasps?" asked Carrots, washing her hands over the sink and heading for the downstairs bath, where emergency supplies were kept.

"Funny little skinny ones," said Cherry. "What Dad used to call Guinea wasps, I think. They got her in the face when she went under a bush. I went first, but I was short enough so I didn't touch it."

"Well, if she hasn't gone into shock by now she probably isn't allergic," Carrots said, half to herself. "So the old snuff treatment should do the trick." She reached for the hump-shouldered bottle. "Get me a big leaf of aloe vera," she called to Cherry. The child's feet pattered away to the porch, where the pots of green stuff lived.

By the time she returned to the kitchen, her cousin had washed her flushed and swollen face in cool water from the sink tap. Her tears were under control. The black eyes were the only feature that could still be recognized as hers.

"Here, sit in Mama's chair," Carrots said. "This will take out the sting and bring down the swelling. Just put your head back against the cushion . . . like that. I'm going to squeeze aloe vera gel onto you, and it'll feel cool. Then I'm going to dab on snuff, and that will sting just a bit. Then you'll feel a lot better."

The eyes rolled wildly, like those of a cow about to bolt, but Miggle sat as directed and held her head still beneath Carrots's ministrations. She flinched as the gel was smoothed on, but then she relaxed. Carrots knew all too well the feel of stings and the relief of that remedy.

When she finished, Miggle looked very strange. Six lumps, which had been angry welts from stings, were now dark brown spots. Two on her forehead, just above the right eye. One beside her nose—Carrots felt sure that was the one making her face swell so— and another on her chin. Two on her right cheek completed the tally, as far as she could see.

"It really does feel better!" Miggle exclaimed, astonished. "You don't go to a physician for such things?"

Carrots was astonished in turn. "For wasp stings?

Goodness no! It's a twenty mile drive, to begin with. Nothing a doctor can do will give you any more ease than what I just did. Unless you were allergic, there would be no use in going that far and paying for an office call. We haven't seen a doctor since Dad died. . . ." Her voice died away.

For the first time, Miggle looked at her as if she were a fellow human being. "What did your father die of? Mine died of cancer, and my mother of emphysema. Nobody has told me what took yours away."

Carrots looked down at her hands as she corked the small bottle. "Dad had a massive heart attack. We got him to town in the pickup, lying on a mattress in the back. He lived for two days. Then he had another one, and it . . . took him. Dr. Grote said the first one had done so much damage he'd never have been able to work again. Dad would have hated that. He was . . . glad to go, I think." She felt tears at the corners of her eyes and turned to the sink to wash her hands again.

"Oh."

Now that that crisis was under control, Carrots turned her attention to lunch. Cherry made the tea while Carrots sliced the tomatoes with Mama's super-sharp, perilous knife. It had been a table knife, in days gone past, made of nonstainless steel. It had been ground down so thin that it could hardly be seen edge-on, and it sliced through tomato skin without even noticing that it was there. Glen said that it could cut your gaze in two. Carrots felt that might be true. It was a thing to be handled by experienced hands, and with it she had a tray of slices in jig time.

Miggle watched the preparations with interest, but before the haying crew arrived she said, "I don't feel very good. I think I shall go to lie down."

"Turn on the fan," said Carrots. "You might want some ice water. You probably have a bit of fever. Stings do that."

She watched the slender figure move toward the stair. Miggle's step was a little uncertain, and her shoulders drooped.

What a way to begin! she thought. Carrots found it in her heart to feel very sorry for Emiglia.

8
Fits and
Fallings-Out

IT TOOK THREE DAYS FOR MIGGLE'S STINGS TO GO DOWN. Once she had looked into the mirror, she refused to come out of her room, even for meals. Only occasional quiet trips to the bathroom, usually after dark, took her from her hideaway. She seemed to think that if anyone saw her in her present condition they'd disown her or something, Carrots thought.

She had tried reasoning, standing in the hall outside the barely-cracked door. (It was too hot to close it entirely and shut off the draft.)

"Listen, Emiglia, we've all been stung, over and over, by wasps and bees and hornets. Once I swam out into the big pond to check on a dove nest that was built there, layer on layer, in one of the willow trees. When I reached up into the branches to pull up so I could see, I hit a wasp nest. Went right up into the middle of them. It's a wonder I didn't drown. I swam back to shore and ran to the house, and Mama coated me solid with snuff and aloe. I looked like something from outer space for a week!"

There was no sound from the room. "We all know how it looks and how it feels. Really, it isn't *permanent*." There was no reply.

Even Mama got no more from their cousin. Her meals were taken in by a pair of angry-looking hands. Mama considered trying to starve her out, but that seemed too drastic, given the jolts Emiglia had suffered in the last week. So they let her be and went about their work.

The east field was baled and all the hay stored in one of the huge hay barns before the showers began, but those only lasted a day and a half. Then it was time to cut the huge hayfield that fronted on the major creek flowing through Bobcat Ridge. That was a week's work for everyone. Miggle was needed.

Luckily her swelling was reduced to normal by then, and she returned to the sight of her cousins. The night before the big cutting, Mama broached the subject of haying to her.

"This is the biggest cutting of the year. Our cows will depend on the hay we get this week for most of their winter's supply. It takes everyone we have and can get to do all that needs to be done. If you work with us, it will mean that we won't have to hire another boy. Not that we'll ask you to do anything very heavy or complicated; that takes the kind of experience that Charlotte and Cherry have had. But you can pull up the pickup while the men load the bales, or go for fresh water, or just generally fill in where you're needed. Do you think you can?"

For an instant Carrots thought that Miggle was going to refuse. Her cheeks flushed faintly, and her black eyes sparkled with something that didn't look like enthusiasm. From her strategic location at the end of the table, Carrots could see her smooth hands clasp nervously in her lap. Then she drew a long breath. The hands relaxed.

"It is only right that I help with your work, if I am to live here," she said. "Tell me what to do, and I will do my best."

There was not a thing wrong with her words. Mama seemed pleased. Cherry took them at face value. But to Carrots, who had been listening with her instinct even more than with her ears, the tone sounded subtly wrong. She told herself that she was imagining things and took herself off to bed early, knowing that the next day would be a rough one.

Sure enough, as soon as milking was done, the equipment cleaned, the floors washed, and breakfast consumed hurriedly, the real work of the day began. Glen drove the pickup, loaded with extra gasoline and water jugs, while Mama took the larger tractor and Carrots the smaller. All headed across the little creek-branch that hid among willows and sweetgum, then up the washed-out track over the ridge running parallel to the one on which the house and barns were set.

Once again Cherry and Miggle were left on their own, this time to freeze the peas that all had worked at shelling each evening, after the day's work was done. The tomatoes had been canned on the rainy days the week before, but there were still enough coming off the vines to supply all the fresh "eaters" the family wanted. The next day, when the hay had cured enough for baling, all hands would be needed in the field.

The shadows from the surrounding wood still stretched long fingers across the big field. Along its western edge the thick woods that lined the creek huddled secretly, bound together with wild grapevine and woodbine and bamboo vines. Glen headed the pickup in that direction, backed to a low point along the creekbank, and off-loaded the water jugs into the shade, half-sunk in an eddy that would keep them cool.

While that was being done, Mama hooked up the drive on her big rig and came over to help Carrots hitch the old sickle mower to her smaller tractor. Then both took off, Mama hitting the heavy Johnson grass along the creek terraces, and Carrots cutting the lighter Bermuda grass growing on the higher edge of the field. The machinery clack-clack-clacked, the tractors muttered and groaned, and rabbits and snakes and insects fled frantically at this invasion of their home territory.

Coming around a curve in the terrace, Carrots heard a whir of wings even above her own noise and saw a bobwhite quail take off from the ground. She braked the tractor, took the mower out of gear, and climbed down to inspect the spot from which the bird had flown. Sure enough, a nest was hidden among the thick grasses. Six pointy-end eggs, smaller than the tip of her finger, lay there. Knowing the bird would not return once the mower had passed over the nest, Carrots took up the saucer of low grass, along with its contents, and set it into the toolbox under the tractor seat. Cherry's pet bantam was sitting; she just might hatch these wild chicks along with her own.

Then it was back to the grind. But for Carrots the job of mowing hay wasn't drudgery. It was something her hands and reflexes could do almost unattended, while her mind soared away into other dimensions entirely. She flew with the buzzard patrolling the field, looking down, in her imagination, through his high-borne eyes at the snorting tractors and the tiny figures guiding them. She made up silly rhymes about the fluttering grasshoppers and the cottontail rabbits.

It got hotter. She began remembering the last time she'd lain on the soapstone bottom of the creek beside her, there in the narrow cut where all the gravel had washed away. It was like a funnel. When the water was running well but not too deep, she could lie on her tummy, chin up to keep her nose above the rill, and feel the coolness flow past as if one were flying through water. The slick blue soapstone . . . she could almost feel it beneath her elbows and knees . . . then the tractor coughed. Coughed again.

Carrots pulled it to a halt and reached down to open the valve that turned the reserve gas tank into the engine. Then she stood and waved at Glen. She knew he'd be along to refill both tanks in another half hour or so. Now—she stared hard at the other tractor—now he had taken Mama's place to let her cool off in the shade for a while. The heat seemed to bother her a lot, these days.

A good half of the field was done by noon. They didn't take the time to go back to the house for lunch but ate sandwiches out of the box Mama had packed earlier. Sitting on the edge of the creek on a big rock that was streaked with red from its iron content and yellow from something else unknown, Carrots dabbled her feet in the water and enjoyed the almost-chill of the shadowy air.

She wrinkled her nose. Watermelon. That meant a moccasin was someplace close by. She tucked up her feet and looked carefully around the edges of her rock, but she could see nothing.

"I smell a snake," she said to Mama and Glen, who were sitting on the roots of a huge maple that leaned at a drunken angle over the stream.

They, too, checked out their surroundings with no result.

"He must be lying up in the shade under the cutbank," Glen said. "We've got to warn Emiglia about moccasins. I don't think they have those in Europe."

Too soon it was time to brave the blazing sun

again. This time there was no escaping into day-
dreams. Dust and prickles from the grass stung eyes
and throat, stuck into the sweat that trickled down
sides and back and front, under armpits and behind
knees. Faces flushed scarlet. Even hats stuffed full of
green leaves didn't keep their hair from becoming
soggy masses beneath the straw crowns.

But by four o'clock the job was done. The worst
of the day's work was over. After this, the evening
milking looked positively leisurely. They raised the
mower blades, loaded the equipment back onto the
pickup, got everything ready to go. Then each picked
a spot along the creek where there was a fairly deep
pool.

It was sheer joy to get the dusty, sticky jeans and
khaki shirt off, to slide into the water in her under-
wear. Carrots ducked under and rose, snorting deliciously. Topwater minnows butted at her waist, and
she could feel the delicate nibbles of small perch about
her ankles. Two damselflies cavorted down the shady
stream, dipping to touch the surface, then circling
high again. On the bank above her head an armadillo
emerged from the greenery, followed by her young.
Shining in the sunlight that struck through the leaves,
they trundled along like clockwork toys and disappeared into a patch of low ferns.

"Carrots! Come on!"

Glen's call brought her out of the water, back into the grungy clothing. As she slipped on her moccasins, she pulled on her shirt and hurried to the truck. It was time for milking.

The tractor joggled up the well-rutted trail through the woods, back over the ridge. It was a relief to climb off and begin the evening ritual.

But the house was ominously silent when Carrots and Mama entered the back door. Cherry's tear-stained face popped over the stair-rail as they came into the hall.

"Mama, make Miggle be good!" She sniffed.

On the heels of that, Emiglia came from the kitchen, her face pinkish with emotion. "Cousin Ginevra, I must protest. It is shocking to make children do such hard and continuous work. Cherry is only five, after all. She had been convinced that this is the way it is proper to live. She will never make a lady. I don't even mention Charlotte, who is lost to anything decent already. But there would still be hope for Cherry, if she were sent away to school and taught how civilized people behave."

Mama was tired and hot and her blood pressure was elevated by her hard day's work. This was too much. "Civilized people earn their keep. Civilized people do not expect all lifestyles to conform to those they are used to."

She looked at the girl sharply. "Do you have supper on the table, as I asked you to?"

Miggle looked sheepish.

Cherry piped from above, "I made sandwiches and iced tea. Miggle said she wasn't anybody's servant."

Mama turned even pinker than the heat and her blood pressure could account for. She looked sternly at Miggle.

"Emiglia, there are certain things you need to know about living as part of this family. The first is that you are expected to see what needs to be done and to do it without being either asked or told. None of us really enjoy some of the dirty, difficult jobs we have to do. But they are necessary, and we all do them, right down to Cherry, who understands that what she does helps us all to survive. We have no time and no energy to devote to childishness, and a lack of willingness to do what you can to help earn your way is just that."

Miggle turned even redder than Mama. Her mouth opened to protest, but Mama spoke first.

"We have been working hard in the heat. All day long. You have been sitting in the relative cool-

ness of the house. We have four more hours of work
to do before we can stop for the day. Do you think it
is fair for you to expect us to come in and prepare
your meals, as well as our own, when you have not
worked as we have and have nothing better to do
with your time?" Carrots had seldom heard Mama
speak so harshly to anyone.

"I was reading! Studying, so that I might not fall
behind!" Miggle said.

"Tomorrow you will find out what haying is all
about. You will not be expected to cook, for you will
be too exhausted to hold your head up. As we are
now. Until then I think you should take a sandwich
to your room and think long and hard about what it
means to pull your own weight in the world. About
what it means to be a person who disciplines herself,
does what is necessary without protest, and works
within whatever system she finds herself. You are
highly intelligent, but that isn't unusual in our family.
You have been reared to look with contempt upon
those who work with their hands. That is a highly *un*-
intelligent view. One that I hope you will change,
as time goes by. Your father knew little about such
things and accepted the attitudes of his academic
peers, who seldom know about such matters. There is
a world out here that demands all that you have, and

more. You are no longer swaddled in an ancient culture or ivory-tower surroundings. If you are to survive, you'd better learn about how to live in it and cope with it."

Miggle's mouth closed with an almost audible snap. Her cheeks were flaming. She turned and went into the kitchen. In a few minutes she returned and made her way up the stairs.

Cherry came down as her cousin went up, and went to Mama to put her arms about her waist. "What's a lady, Mama?"

"One who does her level best, no matter what the circumstances," Mama said.

Cherry relaxed. "Oh. Then we don't have to worry about *that*, do we?"

Mama laughed and hugged her. Then she went, steps dragging, toward the bathroom to change into her milking clothes.

9
Trial by Sweat

THOUGH THE HAY THEY HAD MOWN IN THE AFTERNOON wouldn't be dry enough to bale for another day at least, that cut in the morning and subject to the day's blistering sun and dry wind was ready by the next morning. While Carrots was cleaning up the barn, Glen ran the pickup over to the hayfield to check for moisture. His verdict, when he returned, was positive.

"We can get started today. We should have the field done, given good weather, by Thursday or Friday. It'll go pretty fast while we're on the high edge and baling Bermuda grass. By the time we get into the heavy stuff where the Johnson grass is, it will slow down a lot, but we'll be close to the end."

So when Carrots reached the house for breakfast, Mama had sandwiches packed, small water jugs iced and ready, and Miggle's haying gear laid out in the back bedroom. Breakfast didn't take long, for everyone was keyed up and ready to go. Only Miggle hung back.

Thinking about it, Carrots realized that this was going to be something as strange and frightening for her cousin as a trip through London would be to any of the Ramsdens. She felt a qualm as she watched Emiglia stalk into the kitchen, clad in one of her khaki shirts, a pair of washed-out jeans (new ones were entirely too hot), and the wide straw hat with the pink scarf tied under her chin. She looked as if she were going into battle.

Carrots grinned at her. "It's not that bad. Kind of fun, really. You're not going into something terrible."

But as they jounced along on the back of the pickup, she began thinking about the heat. That was going to be the worst thing for Miggle, and there was nothing that could be done about it. However, they were in the field before she could warn her cousin about moving slowly and keeping in the shade as much as possible.

This time the pickup was stopped in the woods

on the east edge of the field, opposite the side where
the creek meandered. Tools and gasoline cans and
water jugs were unloaded, and each of the Ramsdens
set about getting ready for the day's work.

Carrots checked the oil in the little tractor, filled
both tanks, and pulled loose straw out of the radiator
grill. Miggle watched her as she worked, her eyes big.

"You . . . know how to do all those things, like
a man?" she asked. Her tone was not a little awe-
struck.

"No. Not like a man. Like a farmer, which I
am," she answered. "Didn't your mother know how
to do anything?"

Miggle looked down at the toes of her borrowed
boots. "Maman embroidered beautifully. She was a
gourmet cook. She kept a shining apartment. But
never in her life did she touch anything mechanical.
Even my father did not. He said that he had never
looked beneath the bonnet of his automobile. I did
not know that women and children could do such
things. Only big stupid men."

Carrots chuckled. "*Autre temps, autre moeurs,*"
she said. Emiglia looked stunned, and Carrots grinned
internally. This particular farmer's hobby was languages.

Cherry had finished settling the water jugs in

their places on both tractors. Now she climbed onto the seat Dad had built for her on the front of the big tractor and waited for Glen to begin raking. Carrots climbed onto her steed, also, and set her toe on the starter bar. The machine ground, then caught, and the small tractor grunted into life.

Glen waved her toward the south end. "Hay's lighter there. Won't work the tractor so hard. I'll take a few turns until there's enough to start on, then Mama can rake, and I'll get the baler ready to go. Mr. Newman's bringing his big Ford over in a while to pull the baler, so we can all move at the same time."

She growled away in a whirl of dust and crickets and began making regular sweeps around the lower end of the field, watching closely as her mother had, to make sure that she didn't leave a windrow too near the steep edge of a terrace. After a time she looked up and saw that Mama had relieved Glen. Carrots twisted in her seat and saw the Newmans' low-bodied Ford pulling the baler. Glen was driving that. The pickup was moving behind it, and one of the Newmans' hay hands was pitching bales into the bed.

Miggle must be doing her part. Carrots relaxed and settled into the rhythm of the day.

By noon the upper end of the field was dotted with bales. Looking, you could barely realize how many the pickup hands had already hauled to the barns and stacked. They sat in the shade with Mr. Newman and Saul, his helper, and ate sandwiches and drank cool water. The scent of the hay was sweet, the shade cool as leaves stirred in the light breeze.

Mama turned to look at Miggle. "So how was your first morning as a hay hand?" she asked.

Emiglia was sweaty and dusty, as they all were. Though the pickup kept much of the dust off, it moved so slowly that you didn't make much breeze. She was flushed with heat, and her hair, freed from the hat, was wet.

She gulped a swallow of water before answering. Then she said, "I didn't think I could drive! And it is easy!"

Glen nodded. "But don't mistake pulling up a pickup in the hayfield for real driving. You stay in low gear, and there's no other traffic. Cherry could do it nicely, as she does the tractor, if she wasn't too short to see out. But I have to say that you did well."

Emiglia blushed redder. "But I still think that you should hire men to do this work."

"There's no money," Glen said. He nodded toward Mr. Newman. "If we didn't swap out work with our neighbors, we'd have to do it every bit ourselves. Carrots and I will be going to Al's next week to help him, just the way he's helping us today. That's the only way we can make it."

"But I thought that all Americans were rich!"

"That's the same kind of thinking that thinks all Texans are cowboys," put in Carrots. "Didn't your Dad ever warn you not to buy a horse without looking at its teeth?"

Emiglia looked bewildered; but before anything more could be said, Mama stood and gestured toward the sun-drenched expanse. "Back to the salt mines!"

Cherry was left to nap in the shade while the rest went back to work. As Carrots moved toward the spot where her tractor had been left, she saw Miggle climb into the pickup again.

"If we can keep her going for a while, we may be able to make something out of her!" she said to a passing monarch butterfly. She cranked her machine and turned once more into the scorching heat of the field.

The afternoon passed with terrible slowness. At midafternoon, Glen sent Miggle to the shade with Cherry, judging that she'd had enough for one unused to the climate. And before the tree-shadow had crawled too far across the field, Glen signaled a halt, blowing the pickup horn in rapid toots until both rakers heard it.

They'd done a good day's work. Almost a third of the field was shorn and baled. If the entire thing had been the lighter grasses, they might have finished in two or three days, Carrots thought, looking over the stubble.

Now Mama, Carrots, and the two girls turned their steps toward the house. Glen would work with their neighbors until it was too dark to see, hauling the bales to the barn. Rain was a great spoiler of hay, and even dew removed much of its nutrients.

Miggle had cooled and rested, there in the edge of the woods with Cherry. When she reached the house and Mama asked her, once more, to prepare supper, she looked into the scorched faces of the two who must still do the milking, carrying Glen's work as well as theirs. She didn't object. She did a good job of it, too, for when the milk hands got back (Cherry had done the calf feeding, as well as her own job of keeping feed in the troughs) there was food on the table and a gallon of iced tea.

Carrots bit into the roast, which had been re-heated with yesterday's gravy and canned mushrooms. Then she looked at Miggle and said, "Your mother must have taught you some of her gourmet tricks with food."

Again the girl blushed with pleasure. "I only

took what Cousin Ginevra had left for me to use. I . . . I'm glad you like it."

Supper passed quietly, without even the teasing and joking that usually went on. Everyone was bone-tired, and all went to bed early, without even pausing to read or watch TV. But as Carrots dozed off, she thought this new situation might not work out so badly after all. She wondered what Miggle thought about it.

10
Going Along

THINGS SETTLED DOWN INTO A NEW ROUTINE AS THE summer crept past. Though Carrots suspected that Emiglia had not revised her original objections to their work and their appearance, she said nothing more. She did her part, when asked, though those black eyes flashed, now and again, as if rebellion might be very shallowly buried. And she learned to help with the milking.

This was a great help in haying season, when Glen must go to return the labor his neighbors had contributed. Though Carrots worked with him most of each day, it was understood that she must be back at Bobcat Ridge in time for milking. If Miggle had the equipment sterilized and put together when she came in, it made things go much faster and more smoothly.

So things plugged along like an old mule, sometimes easily, sometimes balkily, until haying was done for the year. August had set in, and the rains, as usual, had deserted the land. It was too hot to mend fence or anything else. In the mornings they tended the late garden while Glen checked the pasture and worried over the level of the stock pond. In the afternoons each took his or her own direction and survived the heat as best they could.

Carrots headed for the woods, book in pocket. And each afternoon Miggle seemed to become more and more curious. At last she caught Carrots as she stepped from the back porch.

"Where is it that you go every day?" she asked.

"Woods," Carrots grunted. It was too hot for many words.

"Might . . . might I come with you? I've never been, except on the way to the fields."

For an instant Carrots was tempted to say no. Then she thought of the long days Miggle had worked in the hay, the longer hours in the dairy. "Sure."

By now Miggle knew to put on a hat, long pants,

and to get a stick before she set out into the woods
and fields. She bent to pick up her favorite snake
stick, a twist of rattan vine she'd found beside the
creek, and settled her hat.

Feeling rather important in her role as guide,
Carrots took the lead, following the track until a dim
trail forked from it beneath a big hickory. "This goes
right back into the woods. It's a deer trail. See the
prints?"

Though Miggle stooped and peered closely, she
seemed unable to see the small, sharp hoof tracks in
the powdery dust. Carrots supposed it must be a
matter of knowing what to look for. "Never mind. I
probably couldn't find my way around Piccadilly."

Miggle giggled. "Neither could I." She laughed.
"I was never allowed to go out alone. It was too dan-
gerous for a child to go about without an adult."

Carrots parted a clump of dusty ferns and took
up her woods gait. "You remember what I told you,
right at the beginning? About being safe here?"

Miggle hummed agreement as she bent to miss
the tangle of huckleberry leaning over their way.

"It was true. You can see that now, I think."

The younger girl stopped in the path. A clump
of ironwort stood waist high in the patch of sunlight
left by a falling dead tree. Its fringy purple blossoms

seemed to light up the wood. Just beyond, a golden-
rod gilded the spot where a trunk had split from its
roots.

"Oh, do look!" she gasped. "How beautiful!"

Carrots looked, nodded, and grinned. "Just wait
a few minutes. You'll see something prettier than
that."

They moved up the trail. The heat was intense
in the woods, but it had a different quality from that
of the fields. The tree-shadow was soothing. The
scent of the hot leaves and blossoms and dust was almost intoxicating. And then Carrots stopped and
brushed back a clump of hawthorn, revealing a tiny
path that branched from the way. Miggle went
through.

They were looking down into a deep cool cleft
where a series of stony outcrops served as steps down
into the creekbed. The banks were emerald green
with moss. There was the gurgle of water in the dimness, and damp cooled the air. Ferns hung from the
overhanging walls, fresh and unwilted by the heat.

"There's my sitting rock," said Carrots, pointing
across the thread of water that trickled along the
rocky trench. "Come on!"

The rock was big. Bigger than an armchair.
Plenty big for two girls to sit on side by side, while

they looked about them at the wonders of the place. It, too, was upholstered with thick, springy moss.

"Tuck up your feet," Carrots cautioned. "Moccasins love this place almost as much as I do. I don't smell one right now, but that's no sign one won't come. Look! Over there . . . a jack-in-the-pulpit. They're supposed to bloom in spring, but this place is special. It's as if the seasons get all mixed up here. See that vine back there behind us, where the cut widens out?"

Miggle twisted to look. She nodded.

"In a while we'll go and look for muscadines. They're the native wild grapes—they and sandhill grapes and fox grapes. But muscadines are . . . are *luscious!* They always make big crops here, no matter what the weather does. It's the water."

Carrots pointed into the deepest shadow beneath a rocky overhang. "Can you see a sort of glimmer back there?"

Miggle nodded.

"That's where the water bubbles out of the rock. This little branch starts right here, and it doesn't go very far through the woods. You can drink this water; but don't *ever* drink free-running water anywhere else in this part of the world. It's not only polluted, but it's full of mosquito larvae. Anyway, there's always water here, let the rains take as long as they want to. Look over there. . . ."

Miggle followed her gesture and hugged herself with delight. A flock of pale yellow butterflies had settled onto the wet mud of the creekbed and seemed to be enjoying the moisture. Among them was a big monarch. Just above them a spire of scarlet blossoms angled from the bank. It was a picture worthy of a painter.

"And there. . . ." breathed Carrots.

Miggle once more followed her finger.

A terrapin was bumbling along through the short ferns at the edge where the bank met the rocks. His neat shell was patterned in gray-green and brown, and his face was thrust forward stubbornly. He had a mulishly determined expression that sent Miggle into a fit of laughter. He gave her one disgusted look and turned to go into the ferns.

Hugging their knees, the girls waited for the next act in this constantly changing and continuing play. It came in the form of a flock of tiny yellow-spotted birds that settled into the branches of a pine tree a few yards from their perch and began a spirited conversation. A quarrel developed and was settled when three of the number moved to an adjacent tree. Meanwhile, a big blue jay sailed beneath them and stepped into a shallow pool formed by a depression in the rocks. He splashed and sputtered and bathed and drank, while the two girls watched, holding their breaths.

After a bit, Carrots led Miggle to a larger pool, where minnows and tiny, transparent crawfish went about their business in ten inches of water. Into the clay between the red rocks the crawfish—or their parents—had dug their tunnel-like burrows, building chimneys of rolled dabs of clay. These thrust from the water some three to five inches into the air, and Carrots pointed down the throat of one. There her cousin could see just the pincers of a big crawfish.

"You tie raw bacon onto a string and drop the end down in there. He'll catch onto it with his nippers and you can jerk him out and land him," Carrots said.

"Why?"

"Oh, you can use them for fishbait. Or you can eat them, if you can get enough at one time. But you have to put them in a tub of clean water for a day or two first, so they clean the mud out of themselves." She looked about. "We'd better check the muscadines. It's too early, but there are usually a few ripe ones by this time. Then we've got to go. Milking time."

Miggle groaned as she followed Carrots toward the clean-washed space below the tangle of vines. Sure enough, a few dark-purple grapes lay there. At the first taste, Miggle smiled. And Carrots knew that at least one native product of East Texas met her difficult test of quality.

There were enough of the muscadines to put a few in their pockets for the others. By the time they climbed from the cleft and were on their way back toward the house, Carrots could hear the long "Soooooo!" as Mama called to the cows.

"Milking . . . it's awfully regular," said Miggle from behind her.

Carrots had often thought the same thing. But she replied, "Well, I guess it's the way Dad always said. Living's regular, too. And when you're in our business, that's the way it is. But there are so many things we have that people who aren't farmers don't have a chance for!"

There was a silence behind her. Then Miggle said, "I didn't believe that at first, but now . . . perhaps you're right."

Carrots swung her stick to clip a thistle stalk that had cropped up in the field beside the track. It was neat to have someone to walk the woods with. It was interesting to teach Miggle about things.

Was she beginning to grow up? Was this feeling that was growing in her for her cousin the beginning of the thing Dad had told her about?

She whistled sharply between her teeth, letting off steam. Mama's double-note whistle came in reply. Suddenly, heat or no, it seemed to be a perfectly beautiful evening.

11
The School Bus War

INEVITABLY, AUGUST DREW TO AN END. THE BEGIN-
ning of school was upon them. Carrots had mixed
feelings about the matter, as usual. She loved learning,
but she felt that she got just as much done on her own
as she did in school. Different things, of course, but
valuable and fascinating, just the same. There seemed
to be so much time-wasting in school. She kept a
book in her pocket at all times as her defense against
boredom.

    Cherry was, of course, excited, for this would be
her first year of school. She had arrived at the age of
six just in time to be eligible. Mama had refused to
send her to kindergarten: the school was too far away

for buses to run a special schedule for the tiny children, and Mama contended that a six-hour school day, plus a very long bus ride, was too much for a five-year-old. They'd all taken turns teaching Cherry her letters, and she had figured out addition and subtraction for herself, using nuts and bolts that Dad had laid out to use. Now she was going to a real school, and it seemed a terrific adventure.

For Carrots, the worst aspect of the whole thing was riding the bus. By the time it reached their stop, down by the road, it was usually pretty well loaded, for it began its run at Melody, a small hamlet whose school had been gobbled up by the larger school district of Larkin. Melody was inhabited by old-timers who prided themselves on their toughness.

Carrots had braved the bus alone all her school life until now, and she had offered a pretty tough target herself. She'd been left alone, for the most part. But now she would have Cherry to think of, as well as Miggle. She had a hunch that Miggle, by her very look and bearing, was going to draw trouble as honey draws flies.

The first morning, Mama took them to school herself, as was her habit. She liked to meet teachers, get things settled. With Cherry just beginning in elementary school, she wanted to see her safely ensconced in her first grade room before leaving. That helped some, but that afternoon they all had to ride the bus.

Horace Latimer was the driver. He'd lived in Melody for sixty years, knew the parents of every one of his charges, and believed, as they did, that "Kids has to tough things out." That meant, quite simply, that bedlam reigned in the bus behind his stolid back. Jackets got hurled out of windows, lunch boxes were hidden, pigtails (there were still a few small girls who wore them) got pulled almost out by the roots.

When Miggle stepped onto the bus, which was almost loaded, there was an instant of silence. Carrots stood and motioned for Miggle to join Cherry on a seat halfway back.

"This is my cousin Emiglia," she said to Mr. Latimer. "She'll be living with us and riding the bus every day."

He nodded, his pale blue eyes taking in every aspect of Miggle. "Foreigner?" he asked, his tone wary.

"She was born in Yugoslavia, and her father was my mother's first cousin. She has lived in London since she was small, so she speaks English as well as we do," she answered. That was a subtle hint for the driver to speak directly to Miggle, instead of behaving as if she weren't capable of answering for herself.

It was too subtle a hint. Latimer jerked his head again, turning his gaze toward the bug-spotted windshield.

As Miggle took her place beside Cherry on the other side of the wide seat, Carrots felt rather than saw a drawing-together among the big boys at the back of the bus. Her neck hair prickled. She gripped her book bag, shifting the contents to make sure the heaviest books were at the bottom, the notebooks cushioned between volumes large enough to protect them.

When Miggle gasped and clutched the back of her head, Carrots was ready. She came off the seat, book bag swinging, and clipped a withdrawing hand sharply.

"Hey!" It was Earl Francis, who wasn't all that mean, really. He just had to prove himself to his peers. Carrots understood that, but she also knew that to let any smallest thing get by without instant punishment would invite more trouble.

"You don't mess with my sister or my cousin. Mess with me, and I'll meet you by the road where I get off! Understand? I don't put up with this kind of thing!" Her voice was grim, and she knew from old

experience that her carroty curls were standing out
from her head in a wrathful halo.

Jeff Enroe, who had covered himself with glory
the year before by holding a terrified first grader out
the window of the speeding bus until a following car
stopped the driver with repeated horn blasts, grinned
evilly. He, too, she knew, was a better person than he
dared let his friends know, but that didn't keep him
from being a terror on the bus. She could intimidate
him, but it was a project she had to work on for at
least the first week of school.

She began her efforts after milking that night.

"Where's my old umbrella?" she asked Mama.
"The one with the heavy wooden handle?"

"In the back closet, I think. I cannot understand
why you want to carry that thing to school every
day. I hoped you'd be out of the notion, by now. It's
like some sort of security blanket!"

Carrots grinned into the darkness of the closet.
Security, yes. But not as Mama thought. She'd never
told her mother about the twin traumas of her day.
There wasn't much she could do about it, and Mama's
day began, now that Carrots must go to school, with
the full burden of milking and canning and calf feeding. If things ever got out of hand, she might call for

help; but until then, Carrots intended to handle things herself.

The umbrella came to light. She dug it out, dusted its faded green plastic cover, extended it fully and thumped the handle into her hand. Good and solid. Just right for thumping heads, and not a few had rung to its tune in the past couple of years. Before that, her red curls had been tweaked, her books hidden, her jackets fluttered from the windows, along with those of the other small ones. But once she got old enough to figure things out, that had changed.

The next day found her loaded for bear. Miggle, in her neat blazer and plaid skirt, climbed the bus step ahead of her, and Carrots heard a snigger from the rear of the vehicle. Cherry got on and perched on the edge of a seat with three other small girls. The bus was so nearly full that Carrots had to stand holding onto the guard rail, facing the back of the bus, while Miggle squeezed into the last seat available.

It wasn't such a bad arrangement. Miggle was as safe as if she were behind a wall, for not a head among those in the rear seats had not rung to Carrots's bumbershoot handle. In fact, Latimer must have wondered at the unnatural quiet that reigned on his bus that morning.

That day school began in earnest. The English teacher must have been pretty certain nobody had read the assignment he'd given the day before: he gave a pop quiz over the first story in the literature book. That amused Carrots. The first thing she did, every year, was to sit down and read through every textbook except for math. She had almost finished the literature book last night. It was her favorite, except for history. She aced the quiz without a hitch. Then she got nervous and wondered if Mr. Garner was one of those teachers who hated for anybody to prove them wrong. She'd had several of those, along the way.

Afternoon came and went, and bus time approached. Carrots felt the shape of the umbrella as a ridge in the bottom of her book bag. She blessed her aunt Ella for giving her one that folded up. Carrying it full-length would have been a nuisance.

This time she got a seat with her family on the bus. Before the vehicle had traveled a half block, a book came flying from the back and caught Cherry behind her head. Latimer didn't look around at her cry of pain. Toughing it out went for the little ones as well as the big.

Carrots took her weapon in hand and set the bag in Miggle's lap. She worked her way down the aisle

to face the four big boys in the wide seat that went
the width of the back of the bus. Without waiting for
anything, explanation or apology, she thumped Jeff
as hard as she could. The *thock* echoed through the
chatter and giggles, and a deep quiet fell.

"Anybody else?" asked Carrots. "I'll keep right
on, if that's what it takes." She retreated a half step
and kicked an ankle that had lashed out at her shins.
Orrie Ewing flinched and tucked his foot beneath the
seat.

"Who made you boss over us?" Jeff was putting
a good face on the standoff. "You're not my ma!"

"You can pitch each other out the window under trucks, for all I care. I won't say a word to stop
you." Carrots sounded as grim as she looked. "But
don't think you can bother any of my kin and get
away with it!" She scowled at them, trying to think
of something from her wide reading that might intimidate this bunch: something unfamiliar and men-
acing-sounding, without being really dirty. And she
thought of it!

"*Figliolo degli diavolo!*" she growled. Languages
were her hobby, and she never forgot a phrase she
encountered in her wide reading. *Little son of the
devil* sounded far worse in Italian than it ever could
in English.

The boys glanced at each other uneasily. They knew they'd been insulted, but nobody knew exactly how.

She grinned as evilly as Jeff had ever managed to do and turned on her heel. No missile followed her back to her seat.

Miggle handed back the bag. Cherry tucked her small hand into her sister's. Carrots sighed and relaxed.

First round! she thought. *And I think I won it.*

12
School Days

THE BUS SITUATION MORE OR LESS UNDER CONTROL, Carrots settled into her winter routine. Mr. Garner, it turned out, was astonished and gratified to find that he had one student who delighted in words. The fact that Carrots was anxious to learn about oddball things and to ask questions that stretched her mind seemed to please him. While many of the other girls pretended to be stupid to keep from standing out from their peers, Carrots forged ahead.

Cherry, in her turn, adored her teacher, Miss Felling, and bored her family almost to tears with detailed accounts of her every word. Miggle, on the other hand, said nothing about either teachers or fellow students. She seemed to withdraw even more inside herself.

It worried Carrots. It worried Mama. They compared notes after the first couple of weeks.

"I know she's bright," Carrots said. "She's passed courses that some of our teachers couldn't. She's reading an awful lot; she's gone through the shelves in the living room and most of those in my room. She's checking out something from the library every day or so, too. But she won't talk about how she's doing, if she's having any trouble because of being a foreigner. Not anything!"

Mama sighed. "I know. I went up to the school last Wednesday and talked with Principal Jared. He sent me to the librarian. Miss Marks wasn't sure she should let an eleven-year-old check out some of the reference books Miggle asked for. It really shook her up when Miggle rummaged around in the old stacks and found Caesar's *Gallic Wars* and brought it up to check out. Miss Marks couldn't understand how somebody her age could read Latin. I think I explained things so there won't be any more problem from that quarter, anyway. Still, I have the feeling that neither Jared nor Marks really approves of children who stand out from their fellows."

"Tell me about it," Carrots wailed. Her mother

smiled. They had had their own problems with the system. Carrots was reading simple French and Latin and beginning Spanish, all on her own, for the school didn't offer languages except in high school. She desperately wanted to begin German, but they hadn't been able to afford the books, and the school certainly hadn't any. The Larkin Public School System taught only Spanish.

Carrots giggled, remembering Marks's shock when she realized that Carrots was checking out English translations of Lucretius and Dante.

"Unsuitable for a child her age!" she'd snorted.

Mama had made a dangerously quiet remark about perhaps the school's wanting to limit girls of her age to Nancy Drew, and Miss Marks had blushed beet-red and capitulated. Chill politeness marked Carrots's visits to the library; but they were frequent, nevertheless.

It was Miggle herself who finally broke her long silence. One evening, some six weeks into the school year, she tapped on Carrots's door.

Cherry opened it, to find Miggle in her red plush dressing gown and fuzzy slippers. "May I come in?" she asked. Both sisters nodded and pushed aside homework to make space for her to sit at the study table.

"It has occurred to me,"—she looked at Carrots,

then away—"that you may well have had some of the problems that I am facing. I understand that you, too, want to learn things not offered in the school. You, too, read unsuitable things. I am always at cross-purposes with the teachers. The other students seem to resent me because I know the material they're studying. There isn't one subject that I haven't covered, and in considerably more detail. I am bored silly. And I'm tired." Tears lurked around her eyelids.

Carrots propped her chin on her knees and thought deeply. Suddenly her head came up. She snapped her fingers.

"I think I've got it! If you're already past all the stuff in sixth grade, we just might be able to test you out and put you in seventh! And Mr. Garner doesn't mind people who want to learn. You could be in the same class with me, and we could tackle new things together. I think Mr. Garner would go for that. I know Mama would. Let's bounce it off her right now!"

Needless to say, Mama was enthusiastic. She promised to go and see the principal at once to make necessary arrangements. "But it's going to make Jared livid!" she warned.

Carrots dozed off that night with the feeling that she had done a good job for everyone. And the next

evening Mama announced that she'd managed to per-
suade the principal that such a move would be best
for everyone.

"He didn't like it a bit," she said, her mouth
wry. "But he knew that I don't stand around with
my thumb in my mouth when it concerns the well-
being of my children. After I went to the school
board about that fifth grade teacher—what was her
name, Carrots?—who tried to fail you for the semester
after you proved that she was wrong in some of her
history, Jared has walked softly around me. I don't
ask anything unreasonable, and he knows the Board
understands that."

So the thing was done, very quietly and with no
open comment. After that things settled down at
school, and a new routine smoothed out, with milking
and harvest and the other regular work that must be
done after school hours. Though Mama and Glen
must bear the brunt of the farming during the week,
things were soon running as well as anyone can ever
expect them to do on a farm, where the unexpected
is always just around the corner.

October was an odd month, every time. Cool
nights and early mornings turned into steaming afternoons, when the sweaters needed on the way to
school became itchy, sweaty burdens. The grass,

dried by the heat of August and September, lost much of its nourishment for the cows, and they had to be given the hay that the family had baled so laboriously all summer. Wild birds and animals were changing to their winter habits and habitats. The school bus often passed foxes and raccoons that had been run over on the highway as they moved around the countryside.

Carrots had always felt restless in the fall. The different scent of the wind, the leaves blowing away their late-summer dusty-green, the entire feel of the world changed for her. The cattle were less placid than they were in summer, too. They butted each other as they waited to be milked, kicked out at those who attached the milkers, just generally made themselves nuisances.

But that was usual. Carrots felt that, considering the addition of Miggle to their lives and schedules, things could have been much worse. New bruises on her shins seemed a cheap price to pay for general peace and quiet.

That, of course, couldn't possibly last.

13
Wolves

IT HAD BEEN A PERFECTLY GORGEOUS SATURDAY. "October's bright blue weather" was paying a visit to East Texas, and Carrots had gone about her work with gusto, reveling in the crisp coolness of the breeze, the brilliance of the sun, and the prospect of a day in the woods, after milking and cleaning were done for the morning.

Miggle, for once, didn't go with her. After suffering weeks of snickers and not-so-subtle hints from schoolmates about her clothing, she had finally capitulated and admitted that her life might be much easier in T-shirts and jeans. Mama had bought what new ones the family could afford and was spending the

morning going through Carrots's outgrown ones.
Miggle had to be there for trying on, and Cherry,
who loved such matters, felt obliged to supervise.

That suited Carrots down to the ground. On a
day like this one, she wanted to run up hills as fast as
possible, smelling the dusty scent of the goatweeds
and rosin-weed. Once at the crest, where the winding
track entered the wood, she slowed to an ambling
pace and breathed long gulps of fall woodsy air. The
mix of hickory leaves, pine needles, sweetgum leaves,
all crumbled together into a rich mulch, combined
into one mellow autumn fragrance.

Carrots swung her stick, riffling a trail through
the leaves as she moved into the wood. She was making for a spot that she always went to visit in the fall.
That seemed the only time of year when she didn't
feel oddly uneasy there. Taking her bearings from a
clump of huckleberry bushes, she pushed through a
stand of young sweetgum and found herself among
big hickories.

She went straight ahead until a corner of gray-
lichened rock thrust up from the mulch. Then she
bore right and found herself standing in a small clearing. In its center stood a hickory—not a terribly old
one, for all its warped appearance. At each junction
of twigs and branches, a tangle of messy growth

blurred the normal hickory outlines of the tree. Almost like nests, the clusters of dead-looking stuff gave the thing an eerie look.

She didn't like that spot at all. It always gave her shivers down her spine. As if something might have happened there, a long time ago, and only the deformed tree carried on the memory of it. She had wondered at times if it might have had something to do with Indians. The Nacogdoche and the Naconi had camped all over this part of the county and had had regular travel routes. Below this part of the wood, down in the flat where the huge ash trees grew, there was the remnant of a very old oak. It was bent at right angles to the ground some four feet above its root. Dad had said that it had been a marker tree for Indians as they traveled on hunting or war expeditions.

She stood quietly, just clear of the overhang of the tree's branches. This was a fit place to meet the fall. It had a faint hint of death in it . . . she shook herself. She never had understood why she kept hunting out this clearing. Once she'd had a nightmare about walking in her sleep and waking to find herself here. That had scared the living daylights out of her. But still . . . maybe it was that everyone needed something a bit frightening, now and then.

Something rustled sharply, coming in her direction through the thick growth of bushes beyond the clearing. She watched as a cottontail rabbit tore across the open space and took to the underbrush again. Something had scared that little guy out of what wits he had.

Turning, she passed the gray rock and the pine thicket beyond it, finding herself on the track again. Its red-clay ruts twisted down the slope between the tall walls of trees. Ahead she could see the white oak that Dad had loved so. Among its thick leafage were specks of scarlet: single leaves turning amid the remaining green. Beyond that lay a glint of sky-blue, the stock pond where she had fished.

She found a spot that was just the right mix of shade and sunlight and settled herself to read. Something unsuitable, of course; she was in the middle of *Candide*, in fact. Alternately chuckling and frowning, she forgot time and sank into Voltaire's oddball view of the world.

The sun had moved to leave her in shadow when she closed the book and rose to stretch the kinks out of her bones. Twigs and gravel clung to her jeans, and she brushed at the mess. It was time to go. The cows would be ready. She might as well swing past the gopher field and drive them ahead of her as she went.

Cutting across the creek that fed the stock pond, she moved along the cut-over neck of woods between it and the field she was heading for. Then she paused, ears cocked. The bawling of cattle came clearly through the trees. A sick feeling filled her stomach. Oh, drat! she thought. The wolves have moved across the pasture!

She could hear hooves pounding into grassy dirt as she got nearer. The herd was running full out, round and round the field. She'd seen it before; they didn't even have to see the wolves as they passed. Just the scent of the pack of southern red wolves drove the cows mad with terror. Some old instinct, left over from their own wild days, she supposed. But what a nasty thing to deal with!

She found the gap into the field. Arming herself with a hickory limb from a fallen tree, she positioned herself behind a trunk just inside the opening and waited for the cattle to come around again. In a bit she heard the trampling and the moaning. Swinging her stick, she stepped from behind the tree, ready at any instant to go behind it once more. A cow didn't even see a person when she had wolves on her mind.

Her unexpected motion did deflect the herd from its round and round pattern. The lead cow dashed through the gap and up the trail toward the dairy lot. Behind her pelted the rest, and Carrots could see that their eyes had rolled until white showed all the way around. They dribbled foam from noses and mouths, and their rear ends were green with manure.

Ugh! It would be a long, long evening. What an end to such a perfect day!

When she reached calling distance, she gave the long whoop that signaled to the others that problems were on their way. Mama's double whistle shrilled in reply. The gate into the barn lot was open by the time the cows got there, and they surged into the enclosure and began milling around in circles, still witless with terror.

Everyone got ready for milking. Miggle, her eyes wide, stared out the milk room window at the filthy forms that whirled past from time to time.

"They are usually so . . . so quiet and docile," she said. "What on earth has happened?"

Carrots set a strainer on a milk can and lifted the milker. "Well . . . don't worry about them bothering you. They won't. Not any worse than this, anyway. But there are wolves that lair in the woods beyond the hayfield in winter. Southern red wolves, to be exact. Very shy; you seldom see one. They just moved their range for the season, and the cows smelled them. It just simply drives them wild."

"Wolves?" Miggle's voice was a squeak.

"I told you, they don't bother people. Really. They're settled into their new home by now, putting a scare into the rabbits. You'll never see one unless someone runs over one on the road. They were here first, after all. They're rare, now. I saw an article somewhere that said there were no wolves left in East Texas. I wish the author would tell those cows that. There has to be at least one pack still left in East Texas, and we've got 'em."

Then they went forth to battle. And it was a battle!

Glen would go out into the lot and put a rope on a passing cow. The beasts had lost any memory of the usual order in which they were milked, and he had to drag each one into the barn, eyes rolling, nose dribbling, tail adrip with manure. Mama, Carrots, and Miggle would push her into her stall and close her stanchion. Then Carrots would hose her down while Cherry brought buckets of soapy water, and the cleanup would begin. They had to wash down every cow from stem to stern before they could attach the milkers. Miggle put the machines on as the cleanup crew moved to the next pair of cows.

Sometimes it took all four of them to drag a particularly hysterical animal into the barn. When they had pushed and heaved and manhandled her into the proper spot, they usually stopped to turn the hose onto themselves, for they were in a worse mess than the cow by the time they had her in place.

The sun went down long before they finished. Eight o'clock came, then nine. By then they had worked the herd down to a handful, and those were calming as they found themselves almost alone in the lot. By nine-thirty things were pretty well in hand. The milking was done, calves fed, the last of the herd driven into a holding pasture.

Carrots faced cleanup with dragging feet. But Mama was pale and exhausted, and Cherry was near to tears with sheer fatigue. So she told them to go on to the house and bathe. She'd finish alone, somehow. She set the milkers and strainers to soak while she hosed down the entire rear part of the barn, soaked it with detergent, and hosed it down again. The smell of manure dwindled to a bearable level. When she returned to the milk room to wash up, she found Miggle standing at the wash vat.

Clean equipment was upended to dry in the usual places, and when Carrots checked, every piece was spotless. Almost everything was done. She found tears rising into her eyes. She was so tired, and this was so unexpected.

"Thanks!" she gulped, helping Miggle lift the cups to hang in their rack, where she turned the spigot to fill each rubber cup with lye water. She'd have liked to say more, but the effort was beyond her.

Miggle looked up at her. She, too, was pale, her black eyes smudged with dark rings of weariness. But she managed the ghost of a smile.

"You are quite welcome," she said in her precise English way. "I felt that you had done enough for one day. I didn't want to come searching and find you collapsed in the path, probably in a pile of manure!"

Carrots began to giggle. Then she laughed aloud, bending over to hold herself. The thought of ending this particular day in such a position was simply too much. Beside her, Miggle was chuckling. They clung together, shaking with hysterical laughter.

Carrots reached to turn off the light. Then they took the homeward path together, whooping at intervals all the way.

Mama heard them coming and turned on the light. As they reached the porch, Roger stared up at them from the mat, took one dubious sniff and went under the house. As they saw their green-smeared clothing and grungy hands and faces, they went off again, harder than ever. This time Mama and Cherry joined them.

Carrots showered in the small bath while Miggle soaked in the large one. Supper, which had seemed impossibly far away less than an hour ago, was now an important consideration. Even as she scrubbed, Carrots's stomach growled.

Later, sitting at the table, she looked about at the others. Somehow it seemed very natural to have Miggle sitting on Dad's bench at her side.

14

The Indivisible Carrots

TIME SLID BY ON GREASED TRACKS. THINGS WERE GOING well, so much so that Carrots had an uneasy feeling that something must be sneaking up from behind. But she had things under control on the school bus. The dairy was going well, with only occasional cases of mastitis among the cows and ill temper among those who milked them. Miggle seemed to be fitting into the family with fair smoothness—or if she disapproved of them she had learned that you couldn't bully a Ramsden into or out of anything. She might hint, tease, or plead, but she no longer went at any of them head-on with her Queen Victoria assurance.

School was no different from its usual self.

Which meant, put simply, that Carrots refused to be a leader and would not be a follower. She went her own way, encased (with whatever book she happened to be reading at the time) in a capsule of self-sufficiency. Intrigues and squabbles among her classmates flowed past her without making any impression. This had worked through six grades of school; she had had no trouble since the first grade.

She had always led any class in grades, effortlessly and without even thinking about it. That had not made anybody happy among her peers, but she didn't worry about that, either. Grades didn't mean anything to her. She wanted what the books contained, and she picked knowledge out as if she were plucking nut meats, then consumed and digested it, made it part of herself. Until Miggle joined her class, she had been the only seventh grader with an average of 99.8. It was a relief when Miggle came to bear some of the resentment generated by such high-performance standards.

So things had gone along as usual, without any really serious ripple in the school waters, until November. Carrots had been noticing vaguely that her girl classmates were looking different. Taller, of course, and beginning to develop what they proudly called "figures." Yet there was something else that she hadn't put her finger on until she came face to face with Louise Fallon in the girls' restroom. Then she realized what it was.

Makeup! The effect of pouter-pink lips and eye shadow on Louise's face almost made Carrots giggle, until she saw the look in the girl's eyes. She so desperately wanted to fit into her group. It was all there: the fashionable faded jeans, the sloppy shirt, both of which contrasted strangely with the carefully made-up face. Carrots longed to pull out a handful of her own self-sufficiency and hand it to Louise, to give her a calm internal balance from which she could deal with the world of school and her mates. But that was impossible, and Carrots smiled as pleasantly as she could manage and waited for the words she could see forming.

For once Louise didn't sidestep in order to avoid her. She stopped and put out her hand. "I've been wanting to talk to you," she said.

Carrots braced herself. From long experience she knew that what was usually wanted from her was help with schoolwork. She didn't mind that, as long as it didn't involve cheating.

But Louise went on, and it took Carrots a minute to catch up with the drift. "It's time we took you in hand. You're a *disgrace* to us all. Anybody would think you don't know you're growing up. It's time you acted like a *girl,* instead of some kind of hermit. We decided that one of us ought to explain things to you. You don't seem to know *anything.*"

Carrots hoped that this was kindly meant, but she found it hard to do. The tone was wrong. The look was wrong. Something rather hot was rising into her throat, but she managed to ask, "And what is it that you think I should be told? About what?"

"About being a woman."

Carrots looked into Louise's eyes. "Heavens, child, my mama told me all about that years ago. I've been a woman, as you put it, since I was eleven."

Louise went brick-red. "That's not what I was talking about. There's lots of things besides the . . . the *biology,* you know. A real woman has to realize . . . certain things." Louise was flustered now and seemed to be a bit more desperate than was reasonable.

"What things?"

"Well, she's got to make herself attractive. To boys."

Carrots couldn't help it. She let out a small whoop of laughter. "To those kids we've gone to school with since we all were six? Who think baseball begins and ends the world?"

"Those are the people we'll marry, one day.

After all, that's what nice girls do." Now Louise was red, splotched with pale spots. Carrots wondered what the problem was, knowing that none of this had anything to do with a real concern for her.

"What century did you grow up in?" Carrots asked. "That's not the only thing open to girls any more. I don't intend to marry. I'm going to write. That doesn't require a husband. If somebody comes along, in time, that I want to spend my life with, I'll do it, but until then I'm not going to worry about it."

Louise squirmed, and Carrots realized that she hadn't reached the point of the conversation even yet. This had all been just leading up.

"A real woman doesn't want to make people look bad. By acting so smart and keeping class averages so high."

Then she understood. Hints and bits of information she'd been unconsciously noting for weeks suddenly wound together into a neat skein. "Oho! James Easton wants to be on the junior team and hasn't worked to get his grades up. But what possible good could my failing something do for him? He could pass on his own, along with several other people I could name, if he'd put his back into studying."

"But if everyone failed English, Mr. Garner

would have to grade on the curve. Then James could make a passing grade without cutting into his practice time."

Carrots knew that the mind that came up with that gem did not belong to someone as relatively straightforward as Louise. There was only one person that devious.

"Margie Sylvester," she said.

Louise jumped. "What did you say?"

"There's no one who could—or would—come up with something like that except Margie. Louise, you know she's spent her entire life plotting and scheming and mixing into squabbles to make them worse. Cheating. Don't think I haven't seen her reading the sole of her shoe. And she's sweet on James Easton. And you're in hock to her for money for the field trip. Put it together and that's how I knew."

Louise looked as if she might cry. "How did you know about the field trip?"

"I'm not deaf or blind." She suddenly felt sickish with pity for Louise. It was ugly for Margie to put someone into such an uncomfortable situation. But it was so like the girl, always a troublemaker, right back to first grade.

"You can tell Margie that I'm not going to get entangled in any of her webs of Machiavellian machinations," she said wickedly. "James will have to learn, like it or not. And as for me, I'll stay a dairyman and a poet and leave being a *real woman* to the experts. And Louise,"—the pale-blue eyes looked into her own for a moment—"don't let her use you like this. You hate it, I can tell. Just . . . don't. That's all."

Louise didn't say anything. She knew when not to argue. She turned and left the room, almost bumping into a girl who was trying to enter. Carrots followed.

What a silly plot, and all to keep a reasonably bright athlete from having to use his head. Carrots almost laughed. Then she thought of something that made her pause in her headlong flight.

What in the world had they planned to do about Miggle?

She'd bet her second-best boot buttons that they'd tackled her, Carrots, first. She was, after all, a known quantity. Miggle, with her British accent, her precise and forbidding manner, was so totally lady-like, so completely feminine, without being in any way like her fellow students, that any approach to her must have looked hopeless. What had they planned to do about her?

The question nagged at Carrots all the way to her next class.

15
The Miggle Caper

CARROTS FOUND HERSELF THINKING ABOUT THAT strange conversation at odd moments. She had known the six girls who considered themselves leaders of the seventh grade feminine contingent all her school life. She liked a couple of them, but none were interested in anything she liked. They squabbled incessantly, but she had seen them backed down by anything that looked even slightly threatening.

Now she realized that she knew very little about them, after all this time. She didn't pick up on their subtle signals or keep up with their gossip. So she hadn't the faintest idea what they might plan to do about Miggle. Snub her? They'd tried that, but

Miggle had snubbed them first. It was a puzzle that bothered her, and she went, at last, to Mama for help.

Mama could see a problem in one breath and solve it in another. Whenever Carrots had argued and protested over one of her pronouncements, it had always turned out to be a mistake, though it rankled to admit it. But this time there wasn't enough information to go on.

"Heavens, I don't know those girls at all. I used to know their mothers, back in the Dark Ages, but I haven't a clue as to this generation. Just watch, Carrots. Have you talked with Miggle about the situation?"

"I tried that. She thinks, poor child, that people are civilized. Except for me, of course. Those girls do all the accepted things that girls are supposed to do, so she takes them at face value. You know, I think she didn't ever know any other children well. She must have gone through school in London or wherever the same way I do, wrapped up in a book so she didn't have to worry about the others."

Mama laughed. "For somebody who claims to avoid people, you certainly notice a lot at times. But you're right. Camilla was so afraid, after they had to leave their own country, she kept her child entirely too close. Even the school she attended was very near her home. She's been grown-up all her life, so it's a bit much to expect her to understand real, gritty, uncivilized children."

Carrots took Mama's advice. When she could, she watched what Louise and Margie and their companions were doing. It turned out to be a good thing. On her way to the office on an errand for Mr. Garner, she glanced down a side corridor in time to see Jennifer Cable closing Miggle's locker. Since all the lockers were fitted with locks, that seemed strange; so when she reached the office, Carrots asked the principal's secretary what she thought about the possibility of someone's opening another's locker without a key.

Miss Jansen frowned. "They're all pretty old locks. There are lockers that you can kick twice and push, and the door will open. How do you know that was your cousin's locker she was closing?"

"It's the one with the big dent in the door. Six down and one over from mine."

"Well, if Emiglia misses anything, you be sure to let me know. We've had pilfering in the past; but I cannot believe that Dr. Cable's daughter would be up to anything except maybe some minor mischief."

Having more than once been enraged by Jennifer's minor torments of smaller children on the playground, Carrots only smiled and nodded. Jennifer might not steal, but she certainly was no saint.

She thought no more about the matter. It was a test day in both math and history, and she set her mind to that for most of the afternoon. When the last bell rang, she scooted to her locker for the books she would need that night. Latimer wasn't patient about waiting for students who showed up late for the bus.

There was confusion in the corridor where her locker was, however. Mr. Jared was shooing students out of the area as quickly as they had finished with their lockers. Aram Davis, the head janitor, was standing in front of one locker as if guarding it. Miggle was standing beside him, looking stunned.

Carrots put away her extra books, got out those she'd need, and went toward her cousin.

"No, no! No loitering and nosing around here! This is purely an administrative matter!" Jared said, making flapping motions with his long, bony hands.

"This is purely a Ramsden matter, for that's my cousin you've got there," said Carrots.

Jared peered at her through his thick glasses. "Oh. Yes. I thought from the start that such unconforming children would be a problem to the school, and I was completely justified in the belief."

"If you'll tell me what's the matter, I'll call my mother and she'll get it straightened out." Carrots made her tone as civil as she could manage.

"Aha! This time your mother *cannot* straighten it out. The police will be here shortly, and they will determine what is to be done."

Carrots felt something cold and greasy in the pit of her stomach. Miggle's name might be Protokiewiescz, but now she was a Ramsden, too. She was family, and Carrots had no intention of seeing her misused in any way. She looked up at Jared. "What's happened? Will you please tell me?"

"Dope," he said with seeming satisfaction. "Marijuana, right in your cousin's locker. She was seen with it, and I was informed. You'd know, a foreigner. . . ."

Carrots flinched. "Where is Miss Jansen?"

"At the dentist's. Why?"

"I was in the office on an errand for Mr. Garner in fourth period. I saw Jenny Cable shutting Miggle's locker and told Miss Jansen about it."

He flushed. "That's entirely too pat. And a relative, too. No, you're not going to smooth this over. We're going to make an example of her. There's been too much of this stuff floating around this term. Here we have the source of it."

"So you're holding Emiglia? Are you holding me?"

He looked surprised. "No."

"Then who is Miss Jansen's dentist?"

He looked flustered. "Grover. On South Street. Why?"

But Carrots was flying toward the office.

She longed for Mama, but she called Dr. Grover's office first. And once a rather wobbly-sounding Miss Jansen got onto the line, things began to move.

"I'll be there at once. Tell Jared—no, call Callie and get her to take the message. He might not believe you."

Carrots called in the student assistant. Miss Jansen spoke to her, and then Callie turned to Carrots. "I'll tell him. You wait for Miss Jansen. She'll be here in five minutes."

"Mind if I use the phone again? I've got to call Mama. We've already missed the bus."

"Of course. I'll be right back." Callie hurried away, leaving Carrots to call her home, a local call, some twenty miles away.

Mama answered after four rings. "Anything wrong?"

Carrots sighed. "Yes. It may be about to straighten out, but we need you. And Cherry will be worried when we weren't on the bus. I think we'll be ready to go when you get here; but Mama. . . ." She paused. "We might need Uncle Benjamin. Just might, not for certain. I found out what I wanted to know . . . about Miggle, you know? They tried to get her expelled for having pot in her locker."

Mama gasped. Carrots could almost see her dark eyes firing up. "I'll be right there. Glen can meet the bus and reassure Cherry. You hold fast, Charlotte. I'm on my way."

Carrots's knees felt weak. It wasn't often that she truly needed help. Her life on the farm had equipped her to handle most things without panic. But this was different. This time she'd needed her mother. She sank into Miss Jansen's chair to wait.

Two parts of the cavalry were on the way. If Miggle wasn't safe now, she'd never be. But oh how she longed to chew someone up for this and spit them into the wind!

16
Lots of Boom and Wango

IF CARROTS HAD READ A DESCRIPTION OF THE NEXT
hour in a book, she would have enjoyed it immensely.
Unfortunately, she found that living through real-
life drama isn't nearly as much fun as reading about it.

For one thing, she was holding onto her temper
with all her strength. She was hot inside with the in-
justice of the thing those girls had tried to do to
Miggles. She felt certain that any notion of arrest had
never entered their air-filled heads. Then she was
churning with nausea. She had always been quiet and
respectful to her teachers. She wasn't naturally a
rebel, not the violent sort, anyway. Having to face
down the principal had tied her insides in knots.

Worst of all, her faith in the judgment of Mr. Jared was unalterably shattered. He, with his long experience, should have understood at once that a fine student like Miggle wasn't smoking marijuana or taking anything else of the kind. Carrots had watched all too many of her fellow middle schoolers drop from high grades to low as a result of that kind of habit. The first symptom was a plummeting of schoolwork quality.

Even less understandable was his readiness to believe that the Ramsdens would have countenanced such a thing, even if it had been true. The Ramsdens had been here forever, and he had known Mama since she had gone to this very school after her parents had moved to East Texas from their native country. The fact that they were all unusual people shouldn't have persuaded him that they would break the law. Being unorthodox wasn't any crime that she had ever heard about.

As she sat holding down her queasy stomach, Miss Jansen came into the office. Her upper lip drooped strangely, and her eyes were a bit glassy, as they tend to be after having a tooth deadened, but she was walking with determination.

Carrots felt dreadful. "Had he finished with you, Miss Jansen? I'm so sorry. I didn't think that

you might be in the middle of something complicated! I was just so upset. . . ."

The woman grinned lopsidedly. "He'd finished.
We were waiting for the filling to harden. He said I
should just be careful for an hour or so. Now where
is Mr. Jared? We need to get this straightened up as
soon as possible. We don't want some idiot getting
shaken up and calling the police. . . ."

As if her words were a signal, feet came tramp-
ing along the hall. Blue uniforms could be seen moving up the stair to the seventh grade area. Miss Jansen
looked as if she'd have ground her teeth but thought
better of it.

"Come on, Charlotte. We'd better get up there
before something is done that will make trouble for
everyone." She strode from the room, pulling Carrots
in her wake.

The hallway now seemed full of blue uniforms,
though there were only three men in blue there. Jared
was sputtering his story. Aram was standing like a
large brown statue. Miggle looked as if she might
faint at any moment. Carrots marched to her side and
put her arms around her waist. Her cousin sagged
against her as if grateful for the support.

Miss Jansen gave the group the kind of glance with
which she usually froze a troublemaker who had been

sent to the office. "I'd like a word with whomever is in charge!" she said. She did not look toward Jared.

"Not now, Jansen!" the principal barked. "Can't you see we're busy with something important? If you have some question, I'll see you in a moment. Right now I am swearing out a complaint."

"Right now you are about to get the school sued for false arrest!" Jansen glared at the principal. "Didn't Charlotte tell you what she saw this afternoon?"

He stared at her. "You mean . . . she really did see someone at Emiglia's locker?"

"Of course she did. Really, Mr. Jared, you've known every Ramsden that's gone through this school for the past thirty years. Did you ever know one to lie? They did everything else within the realm of mischief, but they'd own up to it in a minute. Think, man!"

He looked startled. "But it was too pat; and a relative—surely it couldn't be true. After all, she says the person she saw was Dr. Cable's daughter."

"Yes. But she told me about it only moments after the fact. If I had been here to begin with, none of this mess would have happened. Now you have the narcotics officers here. Hello, Elbert. How's your mother?" She turned her round brown eyes toward one of the policemen.

"Fine," he said. "Do I understand, Miss Jansen, that there is a doubt that this stuff is the property of Emiglia . . ." He stared at the paper in his hand and gave up on her last name.

"A great deal of doubt. Not to mention a logical gap of large dimensions. Heavens, Elbert, there've been dope problems here for two years now. Poor Emiglia hasn't been in school three months! She rides a bus. She reads all the time she's not in class. When in the name of goodness would she have made a connection? And how could she keep her grades so high if she had? I'm afraid that our principal has been a bit . . . precipitate . . . in his actions." She glared at Jared.

Jared glared back. Everyone knew that Miss Jansen's sister ran the school board with an iron hand. No matter how much friction there might be between Jared and his secretary, he couldn't get away with firing her, and that obviously rankled. More than one student had heard fierce arguments coming from the inner office while waiting for swats or excuse slips.

Another of the officers stepped forward. "Could

we go someplace better than this to sort things out? I think this young lady needs to sit down."

One glance at Miggle's paper-white face told Miss Jansen the same thing. Without waiting for word from Jared, she led the way to the office. As they reached the door, Mama came charging through the double doors leading to the front walk.

Things got rather confusing then. While the adults sorted out matters and flung insults and challenges (mainly Mama and Jared, with occasional input from Miss Jansen), Carrots led Miggle into the infirmary and closed the door. She got a paper cup of water from the faucet and handed it to Miggle.

"Sit down before you fall down," she said gruffly. "I think you've had about all either of us can take for the moment."

Miggle's eyes were huge over the rim of the cup. When she lowered it she said, "They did it, didn't they? The ones you were trying to warn me about. But to have me *arrested!*"

"Oh, they didn't think that far. Those bubbleheads just wanted to get you thrown out of school. That would have left only me, and they evidently think they can do something that I'll abide by. Fat chance! No, it never occurred to Margie and company that marijuana is an illegal substance. They use it in the restroom. Didn't you ever smell that awful stink after they've been in there?" She grunted. "They just stuck some into your locker and told Jared and knew that he'd fly off the handle. The way he always does."

Miggle looked sober. "I have never wanted to be friendly with them. It is, perhaps, my own fault that they hate me so much."

Carrots made a rude noise. "It has nothing to do with you, Miggle. Not as *you*. Margie has little projects going all the time, and this one just happens to be getting James Easton on the team without his having to study. Your grades are in the way. Mine, too, and Margie must think she can figure out a way to handle me. But she's never gone this far before. Trying to hurt one of my own folks is something she's going to regret, believe me!"

Emiglia leaned against the wall behind the cot where she sat. She was pale, but her big dark eyes were glowing. "You really mean it. I belong to you, to your family. You stood up to the principal as if I were Cherry." She sighed and looked down. "I know that I have not been terribly easy to live with. I cannot quite understand how you can feel so."

Carrots sat on the round stool beside the cot. "Well, if it comes to that, not one of us Ramsdens is all that easy to live with. We're hardheaded, a bunch of rugged individualists. There've always been fireworks from time to time, even when Dad was with us to smooth things down. But we pull together when things get rough. And Miggle . . . you've been pulling right along with the rest of us. I know you don't really like it. I don't blame you, really, for it's not what you're used to. But you do belong to us. Fights and all. That's what a family is, didn't you know?"

Before she could reply, there came a tap on the door. Callie said, "Your mother is ready to go. It's all settled, I think, though goodness knows how they're going to explain all that pot."

Carrots giggled. "You can bet your socks they're not going to mention Jenny Cable," she said.

Miggle got to her feet and reached a hand toward Carrots. Without speaking they went to join Mama.

17
Midwinter
Mullygrubs

WITHOUT EVEN SPEAKING ABOUT IT TO EACH OTHER, Carrots and Miggle went back to school the next day grimly determined to put spokes in the wheels of the Sneaky Six. The best way Carrots could think of to do that was to ace all her six-weeks tests. Evidently Miggle had the same thought, because both made straight hundreds right through the list, except for one 99¾ for Carrots, caused by a misspelled word. (Their school had gone back to counting off for spelling, no matter what the test.)

After that, there was no more talk about grading on the curve or getting James onto the team. Margie had gone on to other things, anyway. This time she had begun agitating to get the PE teacher fired on some ridiculous pretext, which boiled down to her forbidding smoking of any kind, anything, in the gym showers.

And James, freed of his too-ardent helpers, buckled down and made straight Cs on everything and made the team without trouble. That tickled Carrots a lot; she had known he could do it all the time.

But now it had settled down to being winter, as only East Texas can do. Not a frozen winter of snow and constant cold, but alternating rain and northers and muggy weather and then more rain. Frosty mornings came seldom, and even then the sun usually disappeared behind woolly clouds before noon. Then even more rain would come mizzling down. The temperature hovered around just-too-warm-for-a-sweater and just-too-cool-for-shirtsleeves.

Everyone came down with nasty colds and coughs, which made getting up in the damp darkness to get ready for school even more miserable. And the evening milking degenerated into a messy scramble among wet and ill-tempered cows. November slogged along, getting worse and worse. Only the approach of Christmas gave any hint of light ahead.

Carrots had decided to become an astronaut, leaving behind her any chance of rain at all, as she bent to put milkers on Clara. As always, she was keeping a corner of her glance on the big cow's ears and the one visible eye. Clara was a kicker, when she felt she could get away with it. Shoulder squished into the soggy hair of the cow's side, Carrots set the cups, tested their stability, and straightened to stretch her back. One cup slipped, and she swooped to catch it.

A fatal mistake. Seeing her chance, Clara lashed out with the kind of sidelong swipe that only a cow can achieve, sending Carrots flying beneath the belly of the next cow in line, then on against the wall with a thump that shook the building.

"Hey! You all right?" yelled Glen from beneath the cow he was stripping out into a small bucket.

Carrots gasped, her lungs straining to get some air into them. It was like trying to breathe through a stone wall.

"Ugh! Ugh! Ugh!" she grunted. Then her lungs expanded a bit, and she pulled in a grateful breath.

Wow!

She straightened gingerly, feeling along her bones for damage. Shoulder okay. Arm . . . sore and bruised, but movable. She took a deep breath, and a pang went through her. Right in the middle of her upper chest something seemed to be wrong.

Mama was beside her now. "Trouble?" she asked.

Carrots nodded and touched her breastbone, just below the collarbone. "Here."

Mama touched her with firm but gentle fingers. Three spots of terrible soreness throbbed into life. "Ah." Mama caught her right arm and maneuvered it behind her back, then shifted it forward and twitched it. A triple thump, silent but quite plain to every nerve, marked the repositioning of her topmost three ribs into their sockets. The pain was still there, but it lacked the knifelike urgency it had had before.

"You let me do the bending for a while. We don't want those ribs coming out again. They need to get resettled into place," Mama said, as she attached cups to the cow waiting beside Clara.

It took a week for things to mend enough so that Carrots could do her usual work. She cleaned equipment, helped Cherry with feed, headed off cows who decided to go into another's stanchion for a stolen bite of grain, but her routine was upset. It didn't make her happy at all. A minor case of the doomfuls kept her glum and quiet.

School let out for Christmas at last. By that time Carrots was back to her usual form, but the gloom of the past days seemed to hang onto everybody. Even Mama wasn't full of her usual fizz of Christmas activity, though she had the tree up and the house decorated according to family tradition. Even the smell of Christmas cookies lacked something it had held in years past. It was as if everyone might be waiting for something to happen, some catastrophe to fall from the winter sky.

A big box came from Aunt Lizzie. One of the Christmas routines was waiting for the UPS truck to arrive with the annual treat. The big brown truck came on schedule on December 20. Bigger than usual, the box required Mama, Carrots, and Cherry, all three, to manhandle it into the house. It was filled to the brim with wrapped packages. They went around the tree at once.

Lizaveta, like her niece, loved Christmas. Carrots knew that their own gift box from Texas brightened the lonely old lady's holiday season more than any expensive gift might have done. For the Ramsdens filled a heavy carton with holly, from the big tree in the west woods, packing its cut ends with dampened moss from the creek. Sweet potatoes from the garden, peanuts from the big field they always planted, thickly

wrapped jars of plum and berry jam and sandhill
grape jelly went into the box, together with homemade things like crocheted foot warmers and cross
stitched dish towels.

Lizzie wrote that she invited tenants of the
neighboring apartments into her home for the opening of The Box, every year. They roasted peanuts and
sweet potatoes, made sandwiches of jam and jelly
with butter, shared out the crisp holly among all of
them, and caught a distant whiff of a way of life that
few of them had ever dreamed existed. Carrots loved
to picture in her mind that instant of communication
that took place each year between her wild and
woodsy home and that cramped world so far away.

Miggle seemed at a loss. A family's Christmas
routine is so individual that no outsider can quite fit
in or even understand why many of the things that
seem so important to those involved are done at all.
Her puzzled glances at the battered angel on top of
the tree amused Carrots, once she noticed them. That
angel was no beauty, that was certain. A loop of tinsel
would be much prettier, in point of sheer appearance.

Catching Miggle gazing up at the tree, Carrots
said, "I can see that you think we ought to throw out
Gabriel, up there, and put up something younger and
prettier."

Emiglia shrugged. "It seems . . . a bit odd. I should think something less threadbare would look nicer."

"Not to us," Carrots said. "That was the very first ornament Mama and Dad ever bought for a tree, just after they married. It's been on every one since then. See that dent in his forehead? That's where I dropped him, the first time Dad held me up to put him on the tree. And the stain on his robe . . . that's where Glen's finger bled on him. He'd cut it on a broken glass ball. Every scar that poor angel has means something to us. You know, Glen has bought one for Chuck, this year. He and Millie intend to do the same with it as Mama and Dad did with this one. Make it part of the family."

Miggle stared up at the dingy shape at the tree-top. The colored lights reflected in her black eyes with myriad flecks of brightness. A tear at the corner of her eye reflected still more. But she didn't cry.

She looked at Carrots and said, "Oh, yes. I remember Mama and Papa had a spun-glass bird. It had been broken, probably when they packed so hastily to leave Yugoslavia. But they got it out every year and propped it up on the mantel, with a nest of greenery about it. It meant something to them, I could see that, but they never told me what. I wish I knew . . ."

An overwhelming sense of sadness came over Carrots. She stood in the middle of a family. Even with Dad gone, she had all those memories of him and his tales and his games and traditions. But not only was Miggle in an alien place, surrounded by people who didn't speak as she did or think as she did, but she didn't have the comfort of knowing all the funny little family things her parents had shared.

What a lonely thing it must be! She moved closer and put her arm about Miggle's shoulders. Together they stared up at the tree. Cherry came to wriggle between them and stand, too, her plump little arms straining to reach around both.

18

It Was a Dark and Stormy Night

CARROTS WAS THINKING ABOUT SNOOPY'S INEVITABLE beginning to his comic strip novels as she washed Half-Pint's udder. Warm drips ran from the cow's back onto her own. Outside, thunder growled and grumbled menacingly, and the evening had turned dark as midnight, long before the usual time for full darkness to fall.

She finished that pair of cows and turned to the big sliding door. It rumbled back on its track a bit, but the noise from outside was so loud that she couldn't hear it. Something was clattering onto the tin roof with deafening din, and suddenly, before she could get the door open, the interior of the room was filled with swirling dead leaves.

For a moment she couldn't see across the brightly lit space. The door sucked outward, and she caught the handle and held as hard as she could. A sound like a passing train shrieked even above the thunder of sweetgum-balls battering the roof and blowing between the tin and the walls to join the leaves inside.

It was a moment suspended in time. Her gaze met Glen's, and she could see frantic speculation in his brown eyes. Cherry peered out of the feed room, her round face solemn.

"It's blowing awfully hard, isn't it?" she shouted, and Carrots nodded, suspecting what had just happened.

"Mama?" she asked. Glen read her lips, for the noise was still deafening, though it was no longer that awful shrieking, just the drumming of a torrential downpour on the tin above them.

The door quivered as if someone might be trying to open it from outside. Carrots turned and pushed it along the track. A bedraggled figure stood in the flooding rain.

Water streaming from her hat and jacket, pants and boots, Miggle seemed not to notice that she was wet at all. Her pale face was agitated, and her eyes were huge.

"Glen! The top of the hay barn is partially blown away, and all our hay is getting wet!" She sneezed. "Cousin Ginny is up there trying to move it over into the space where we've used it up, so no more will spoil. It's hard for her, and I'm not strong enough to help much."

Glen rose, handed his bucket to Carrots, and put on his hat. "Help Carrots milk!" he said and strode into the darkness without another word.

In the light from the fixture above the barn door Carrots could see all the cows standing in a tight huddle behind the fence. There had been a new calf in the shed some thirty feet behind the dairy barn. The shed was gone. Where was the calf? But there was no time to worry about it now. She had to milk the anxious beasts that were jockeying for position to get into the dry, bright barn.

Miggle stood back to let the next pair in. Ruby and Iris clattered into their places. You could almost hear their sighs of relief to get out of the frightening night they had left behind them. Carrots washed them; Miggle attached milkers; Cherry brought feed for another pair; Carrots went back to strip out the last two. It was as if they'd worked together for years.

The lights didn't blink. That boggled Carrots's mind. Usually the power went out if there was a tornado. That was something you expected. Sometimes their power went off when there was a hard rainstorm. And here they were, not one blink, after having a twister go thirty feet behind the barn. It was a miracle, and one she was more than grateful for.

How many times had she and Mama and Glen—and Dad, when he was alive—had to start milking by hand? Twenty-five to thirty head of dairy stock that gave from two to three gallons per cow at one milking! Her hands ached to think of it. You milked until your arms felt as if they'd fall off; your hands cramped into paralysis and had to be rubbed and flexed to bring the fingers back into motion. Your back ached with stress; the cows finished their feed and began stepping around, flapping you with their tails, urinating in odorous floods onto the concrete floor.

Usually the lights came back on before they'd had to milk more than half the herd. That was good, for if they'd had to go through the entire bunch it would have been time to start again by the time they finished. They'd been more than lucky, this time. With only Miggle and Cherry to help, willing as they were, it would have taken her all night, and then she probably wouldn't have made it.

She rose and pulled out the peg that held Half-Pint's head securely between the movable bars of the stanchion. The small half-Jersey pulled her head free and turned to look at Carrots with pleading eyes. Carrots tapped on her back.

"I know you'd like to stay in here where it's dry. But you've got to go out. You know very well you can go into the big shed with the rest. It's Holly's turn now!"

Half-Pint sighed as if she understood. Her feet clipped sharply as she backed to turn out of the door. Holly, seeing Cherry ready with a bucket of feed, tried to pass the other cow in the doorway, and Carrots had to get a long stick to quell the impatient animal. As she stepped outside, Carrots looked toward the hay barn. The lights shone steadily—and one wide beam thrust upward through a gap in the roof.

"All that hay!" Carrots sighed, letting Holly past her into her place. "We worked so hard, getting it baled and under cover!"

Miggle handed her the wash bucket and stood watching as she cleaned the udders. "I know. I never would have credited it. I wonder how many people in

London believe that their milk just springs into being in the bottles on the grocer's shelf? It never occurred to me that there was so much involved in getting it there."

Cherry giggled. "Miss Felling said there was a lady on TV who said that she didn't care a hang for farmers. She got all her food at the supermarket, anyway. What did she need with farmers?"

Carrots laughed. So did Miggle.

The rain dwindled a bit, to a steady downpour, then to a quiet patter. The cowlot ran ankle deep in water, and when they had to step outside, the mud came well up on their boots.

"I hope they got the hay under shelter. There was room: we started using it out from under the other end of the barn. But oh, it's a pain to maneuver hay bales at the best of times. Trying to do it in a tearing hurry is miserable!" Carrots stripped out the last drip from the last cow and stood. "We're done. We can clean up fast, if we all pitch in, and then we may be able to help move hay, too."

But by the time the barn was cleaned, equipment sterilized, the light had winked out in the hay barn. Glen's pickup groaned and splattered through the deep mud of the driveway as he headed for home. A prickle of light from a flashlight showed that Mama was on her way up the trail.

"Go and meet her," Carrots said to Miggle and Cherry. "I'll wait here and let you make it most of the way with the light on. No telling what has been blown into our way. My feet know the way all by themselves, and you know I can see in the dark."

The two squished away, tall slender girl holding the hand of short round one. Carrots saw them meet Mama, and the three turned into the path toward the house. When they reached the back gate, she switched off the light and closed the door behind her. It was black as the inside of a cow. Rain slid greasily down her face when she looked up to see if there might be any break in the cloud cover.

Her booted feet felt their way along the soggy ground. Now and again there was a piece of tin or a chunk of wood that didn't belong in the path, and she knew it was part of the barn roof, more than likely. The porch light loomed ahead. She walked faster.

Tonight a hot bath, a good supper, and bed would feel better than good. And tomorrow, school or no school, she knew that she and Miggle must stay home and help Glen and Mama find that missing calf, mend the barn roof, and build some sort of shed for the newborns of the herd.

She stopped at the gate, her hand on the slippery latch. Funny. It was so natural, now, to include Miggle. Maybe you didn't have to be born into a family to become part of it. Maybe you could be transplanted into it and grow your own kind of roots.

"Hurry, Carrots! I've got your bath ready!" That was Cherry, bless her!

Carrots lifted her heavy feet up the steps and turned to gaze back toward the invisible barn. In the sky a single rift in the cloud allowed two stars to peep through.

19
A Family Decision

THE TORNADO CAME WITH THE NEW YEAR, AND IT seemed to clear the air of all the swampy feelings the fall had left. Carrots felt vigorous. Even just mopping under her bed was a thing she put her back into, knowing the stretch of her muscles with sheer pleasure.

School was going fairly well. She and Miggle had relaxed into their usual dedicated paces, and they noted with some amusement that Margie and crew were still waiting for the axe to fall in revenge for their underhanded plot. The two cousins decided that waiting for well-deserved and undefined punishment was much worse than getting it over with, so they grinned fiendishly at any of the plotters who crossed their paths and let it go at that.

Miggle, in putting away her blazers and skirts, seemed to have put away some of her stuffiness. Not all, by any means, and when she felt strongly about something she was required to do but objected to, she made that plain, but she spoke less and less about what was "ladylike." As Mama had told her, to be "like" a lady is nothing. To *be* a lady, strong and determined and ethical, is what counts. Something about that—and the hard work, the sweat, the painful times and the funny ones, capped by that stormy night—seemed to have reached deep into the core of the girl and pulled forward a part of her that had never had the chance to develop.

She grumped less and less. She seemed to resent the work less, too, and to pitch in with far more willingness than Carrots would have thought possible.

Yet in spite of all this, Carrots sometimes found she felt antsy and uneasy with the world, though she was full of ambition and interest in everything she could get her hands on. Mr. Garner, pleased with her efforts at verse, supplied her with books on poetics, as well as his collections of the works of great poets. She read all with varying degrees of comprehension, pleasure, and puzzlement. Then she wrote about things none of the others seemed to have heard of: tractors groaning through summer hayfields; ponds pocked with raindrops and edged with dripping willows; all kinds of things that made up her life.

"Write more about people!" Mr. Garner told her often.

She always shook her head. "I don't know many people. Just family and schoolmates, and they're mostly alike. I'll write about people when I know something about them. Until then I'll keep on with buzzards and crawfish and tornadoes."

The year crawled on toward spring, then summer. School was closing. Another summer of work and woods-roaming was coming, and Carrots found herself hoping her cousin would want to go with her to all her special spots.

The end of school meant the beginning of rising at five to milk again, a matter that brought groans (quiet ones) from Carrots. Yet the fresh mornings were intoxicating, in their own ways, and Miggle decided on her own to help with the morning work. That meant they got through much more quickly.

Carrots found herself wondering how she had managed before Miggle came. She made the work easier, true, but there was more. There was someone to laugh with as they cleaned and scrubbed and hosed down the dairy barn. And there were the many matters that Miggle understood, and now Carrot understood, too. Ways of seeing things that came from living in other countries. Ways of coping with life that, while not exactly to her taste, were nevertheless interesting and probably would be useful in times to come.

As they walked through the dewy wood toward the garden, one morning, she put it into words. "It's fun having you here. I never thought it would be so much fun to have someone my own age, but it's neat. Cherry is too young to catch most of our jokes or to know the people we talk about at school. I have to admit that I dreaded your coming. It seemed as if it would change everything, make home and the farm somehow different. And it has, really, but different can be better. I didn't know that before."

Miggle had a hoe over her shoulder and a sprig of sweetgum twig between her teeth. You couldn't tell by looking that she was the same person she had been those few months ago. Still, there was something about her, something about her walk, her manner of carrying herself, that was uniquely Emiglia.

She smiled. Her pale face had tanned to a golden shade, and her black hair was caught into twin ponytails. She moved through the woods with an easy step, and even the squeal of a rabbit in the brush didn't make her cringe. She began hoeing her row in the garden with vigor, though Carrots knew that she still disliked hard physical work.

Carrots envied her that self-control. She had begun trying to develop it in herself, and she found it a very difficult thing to do. Since those first hard weeks Miggle had never lost control of herself. Once she learned that the family truly depended on all its members for survival, she had done her part, unwilling to be a parasite upon the work of the rest. She had told Carrots as much, once, and it had brought them very close for that moment.

The morning went by, and the garden was hoed. They went to the house with Carrots's hat full of zucchini. Mama had lunch ready when they arrived.

There was an odd expression on her face. It gave Carrots a shiver down her spine. It wasn't a doom-and-catastrophe look. Just strange. Something was afoot.

She didn't say anything before lunch, but afterward when they usually lay down for an hour to read or rest through the hottest part of the day, Mama called the girls into the living room.

"I've had a letter," she said. Something went clunk in Carrots's middle.

"It's from Aunt Lizzie. She has worried about

Emiglia, here in this hot climate, doing work she isn't used to. She has found . . ."

"Another relative!" Miggle exclaimed. "Is that it?" She looked a bit strange, pale beneath her tan.

"Your father's mother's uncle came to this country in 1956. His son lives in California, and he's quite well-to-do. He has one child about Carrots's age. And he has offered a home to Emiglia, if she wants to come."

Carrots blinked hard, forcing the tears back inside. She had no doubt that Miggle would go. She would have an easier life, a better school, nicer clothes. All the things she valued so much. She still disapproved of so many things the Ramsdens did and thought and were.

She was much more conformist than her cousins. She liked doing things in a way she considered genteel. No, Carrots had no doubt what her decision would be.

Mama was reading the letter aloud. ". . . and Charles can afford to give her an excellent education. His and Martha's home is in the San Fernando Valley, a beautiful place from the photographs he sent. They feel that Emiglia and Sarah will find themselves compatible. Charles is well able to give her what she needs without any financial strain."

Miggle was staring at Mama. Her expression was unreadable. When she spoke, her words startled Carrots.

"Do they need me?" she asked.

Mama glanced up, surprised. "From what Lizzie says, I don't think they need much of anything. But they want you, very much."

Miggle dashed a hand across her eyes. "Do *you* need me?" The question was harsh and straightforward.

Mama looked at Carrots, then at Cherry. Both were looking back intently.

"Yes, we do. You have made life easier for us all. Glen has worried about Charlotte and me doing so much, working such long hours at such heavy jobs. It's been a relief to have another pair of hands. But that isn't all. We had lost one of our family. You're filling a place that was empty for too long. It isn't just your work we need, dear, it is you, too."

Miggle smiled. From behind her controlled expression there dawned something Carrots had not seen before in her cousin. A happiness that glowed through her.

"Then if you don't mind, if you can afford it, I want to stay here. With you. I freely admit that I dislike the work. I hate getting my hands dirty, smelling cow manure and sour milk; but there is so much more to life here than that. I like feeling a part of things. A *necessary* part.

"Maman and Papa loved me dearly. I never doubted that. But they thought of me as a kind of pet or adornment to their lives. Never once did either ask me to do something for them. They thought of me as helpless, a mere child, incapable of doing anything useful. Since I came here, I have learned that being a child does not mean that one is useless or helpless. I am making a difference. I am earning my own way in the world, and I have learned from you that it can be done with a style and dignity that my parents would not have believed possible with hard labor on the land."

She sniffed hard. "Besides, I am beginning to be fond of you. All of you. *Quite* fond."

Carrots began smiling. Cherry hugged her tightly, and Mama giggled. There was a bit of sniffing before anyone else spoke.

Then Mama said, "I think I'll go write a letter." She grinned at Miggle. "Cordial thanks and a firm refusal. Okay?"

Miggle nodded, then frowned. "Would it be too much . . . could we ask . . . if their Sarah might like to visit us here? There are so few of us in this country. If it isn't an imposition. . . ."

"Better yet, I'll ask them all to come," said Mama. "A jaded Californian with too much money might enjoy sweating in a hayfield as a change of pace. I'll ask the entire bunch!"

Miggle sighed. Carrots grinned, and Cherry. Roger, peering through the screen door, thumped his tail on the porch.

Carrots thought with amazement of the self-centered person she had been, wanting to fence out anyone new from her close circle of family. Well, now she knew better.

Outside the mockingbird settled into her nest among the climbing roses. Carrots heard her chirp as she came to rest. A cricket, cool in the shade under the Chinese holly, began to shrill. A cow lowed mournfully in the distance.

For this short space, all was right with the world.